Touched

by
Paul Maurer

New Libri Press

This is a work of fiction. Nothing is in it that has not been imagined.

ISBN: 978-1-61469-035-1

Published in 2013 by New Libri Press
Mercer Island, WA 98040
www.newlibri.com

New Libri Press is a small independent press dedicated to publishing new authors and independent authors in both eBook and traditional formats.

Contents

1	The Landing	7
2	Spoon Fed	24
3	Ring of Fire	38
4	Slow Bleed	52
5	A Strange Voice	62
6	In My Head	78
7	Sea and Sand	93
8	Spillover	107
9	The New World	122
10	Round Two	125
11	And Stogies for All	134
12	Aftermath	143
13	Bound and Gagged	153
14	Shadows in the Night	162
15	Thunder in the Distance	169
16	Fallen from the Nest	181
17	Day of Truth	191
18	Black Opals	206

I wish to dedicate this to my wife, Sue, and my three sons, Adam, Jeremy and Luke, for their love, patience, and support.

Secondly, a thank you to my family and friends for their encouragement and thoughtful suggestions. Without your help I never would have made it anywhere close to the finish line. Just as much, a thank you to Michael and Stasa for taking it the rest of the way. Lastly to Charlie and Cele, just because you are you.

Chapter One
The Landing

The volume exploded in my head like a chip gone bad. In a dead-heat for second place was the knot gripping my stomach and the baseball living in my throat. It only got worse when the noise of the lunchroom pierced my skull like the ear-shredding drill of my sadistic dentist with the shitty breath. Then, with my brain on full buzz, she stepped into the room.

She had on a plain white t-shirt and reminded me of one of those butterflies fluttering through blue skies in summertime. She moved slowly and her eyes darted back and forth like she was searching for a place to land. Then she looked at me and smiled. I didn't know what to make of it and was sure she thought I was somebody else. When she smiled again my life went a complete one-eighty.

It was the first day of school, sophomore year. As usual, I sat at the loser table with a couple of nimrods, nosepickers, and Curt. Curt was another high school reject; over time we had formed a nerd-like bond. Nothing like strength in numbers. When she walked towards our table I was sure she was going to punk me so I would look like a total deek. I had never seen her before and was certain she was new in school. As fingers from The Hot Table pointed to her, I knew I was right. She had black, tangled hair that ran down the middle of her back that framed an olive colored face and dark eyes that reminded me of a rock I studied in geography. Anthracite, I thought. Black eyes that kept my look far longer than intended. I looked away and hoped she might disappear to save me from being gutted in plain sight. When she spoke it was in a voice as soft as a baby's breath.

"Do you mind if I sit here?"

I waited to see if she would laugh at her own question. *Did Hitler's mustache make him look like a douche bag?* I wanted to ask in return. Of course she could sit there! Hell, she could sit on the freakin' queen's throne if the school had one in the budget. Pick a chair, any chair. And yet, there she was directly across from me.

"Sure," I mumbled as I worried about what would happen next. "Whatever you want."

She touched me on the shoulder and it was like a spark jumped under my skin. She kept a fingertip there longer than necessary and when my mind jumbled I stayed quiet.

"It's alright," she said as she drew her hand away. "I would never hurt you."

Never hurt me? What the hell did that mean?

She was at most a hundred pounds and even though I was a top candidate for the school's pencil-necked geek, I knew she couldn't hurt me. When my mind got right, I played it a little tougher.

"No shit!" I said in a voice that squeaked more than I intended. "Why would you?"

She shrugged with a smile that confused me. I didn't need a new girl to mess me up more than I already was.

"Doesn't matter," she said. She paused. "Can we start over?"

As paranoid as it sounds, I was still waiting for her to go tell her friends that some dork invited her to stay. But when she opened her milk carton she was there for good.

"Sure," I said. "Why not?"

"Thanks," she said. "I didn't know where to go."

She stopped talking and I waited for Curt to say something. He suddenly found his pile of greasy french fries as spellbinding as a look in the girl's locker room.

"These are the best seats in the place considering the food. Near the bathrooms," I said lamely. "I'm Jimmy. And this is Curt."

"Nice to meet you Jimmy. You too, Curt," she said with a nod. "I'm Renee."

Curt nodded politely but didn't say a word. He was leaving it up to me to talk. It's not that I think of myself as a debate expert, but at that moment I developed an instantaneous case of full-on high school lockjaw. I never had a girl looking like her, care about talking to someone like me. In fact most girls under a quarter ton would look through me like I was a hundred and twenty pound piece of scotch tape.

"I d-don't recognize you," I stammered as I patted down my eternal cowlick. "Are you new here?"

She paused and looked over the cafeteria. I thought I said something wrong when she took a long time to answer.

"Yep," she said. "I'm new. Again."

I wasn't sure what she meant and even less sure I should ask her. At worst I figured all she could do was tell me to pound peanut butter.

"Again?" I asked. "What does that mean?"

I was surprised when she looked me square in the eyes. I guessed she was going to unload a dump truck full of monkey dung on me for prying but she answered slowly.

"I just moved in. This is the third year in a row I'm at a new school. Only this year I'm living with my aunt. My mother is …" she said. She took a drink of her milk before continuing. "Anyways, I'm with my aunt now."

She said it in such a way it seemed complete. Then almost instantly I turned into the big mouth guy on TV infomercials that couldn't shut up.

"So you're new to Wisconsin?" I asked as I wiped mayonnaise off my chin. "Where are you from? I mean, the last time."

"You sure are full of questions," she said. I reddened and suddenly hoped for the bell but she kept on. "Nebraska. Land of cattle, corn, and horny cowboys. All totally overrated in my book. Especially the cowboys. And before that San Diego. Like I said, I've been around." When my eyes widened, she continued, "So to speak."

Curt woke up and spoke for the first time. "I've been to California. I tried to surf and split my head open on the board. I had to get fifteen stitches. Left a major scar. Want to see it?"

Renee coughed on her milk and smiled. A real smile, not one of those fake ones that supermodels flash as if they are computer generated. It was then I first believed there was a chance we would be friends against odds bigger than winning the Lotto.

"No, Curt," I said. "We'll keep your scar under wraps until a special day. Maybe her birthday."

"I'm sure it's a nice scar," she said with that smile again. "I look forward to seeing it."

Curt nodded and dipped the last of his fries into a little container of ketchup. "Whatever," he said, clearly annoyed. He took turns looking at both of us. "I'm not a retard you know."

Renee looked almost alarmed. "I never meant to imply anything like that," she explained. "I'm sorry if you took it that way."

He pouted for a second until a satisfied look crossed his face. "Apology accepted," he said as he snarfed another fry with a big glob of ketchup hanging on by a thread.

That second Renee looked like she wished she had never sat down next to us. I struggled for the right words to rescue the situation but came up empty. I even chewed an extra number of times hoping to avoid saying something stupid. Luckily, I got bailed out when she spoke up again.

"So what's this school all about?" she asked in a soft voice. "Is it any good?"

I didn't know how to answer that. Like most schools, it depended on where you were sitting; in the back of the school bus or from the driver's seat of daddy's tricked out SUV. Either way, guys like Curt and me ended up as bugs pancaked on the front windshield. With apologies to Charlie Darwin, I thought of high school as survival of the prettiest.

"It is what it is," I said with a shrug. "The battle plays out daily."

"And that is?" she asked.

"You really want to know?"

"I may as well find out what I'm getting into," she replied. "That way I can avoid any major social landmines."

"Good luck on that," I countered. "It's a warzone if you're not on the right team." Then I took a breath and started in on my dissertation of the school's pecking order. "The 'Billys' rule most of the place. That's what the jocks call themselves. It's a stupid name, but it's in honor of some all-state football player who died in a car crash a few years ago. He was a legend—his brains splattered on an oak tree after he sucked down most of a quarter barrel. Drunk as a mother."

"Nice," Renee said. "A special memory for the school. What about the others boys?"

"Most I call the 'Wafers'. As in 'nilla. Nothing distinguishing if you know what I mean. School, work, and everything else. The ones that will probably rule the world someday."

She carefully closed her milk carton. "What about the girls?"

I was warming up now and licked my lips. "They're even better. Most of them are split into the 'Beez' and the 'Bettys'. The Beez are all the hot ones. Supposedly they got their name because they claim they're 'sweeter than honey'. The other story goes it's just a shorter version of 'Beyonce'—they like to think they're as hot as she was before she got knocked up. I think the Beyonce thing is funny though given the school is ninety-seven percent white in the first place. Anyways, they swarm around like a bunch of mascara-drenched piranhas waiting to strike at any time."

"Looking for fresh meat," she added.

"Exactly!" I replied with too much volume. "Turns out if you're a cheerleader you are still pretty much in the Beez even if you're a little fat."

She nodded as if she understood. "Who's the queen bee?"

That one was a softball. "Veronica Styles," I said. "She's the one standing at The Hot Table giving everyone a show." I pointed to a distant table and worried Veronica was reading my lips as she looked my way. A shiver ran down my spine when she sniffed the air like a bloodhound and narrowed her eyes. Even so I couldn't help admire her usual body-hugging outfit that made us horndogs sneak a look every chance we could. It was like she was carved out of life-sized bar of Ivory soap with all angles and curves in perfect porcelain symmetry. Like a faultless Michelangelo sculpture of teenage hotness dripping with juices waiting to be lapped up by the closest dude in heat. I had never even spoken to her, but one day might be granted the privilege. "You'll see her ruling over her loyal subjects at the sophomore pole just about every morning before school."

"I see," she said almost to herself. "Cute."

"Don't she know it," I replied. Just the thought of her tight body made my mouth water. No disrespect to that Russian guy Pavlov and his dogs, but at least the saliva loosened the remnants of sandwich that coated my upper incisors. Then I continued. "Although there's no absolute ranking system in the principal's office, I'm sure Veronica is the head of the Beez. She's the first sophomore ever to be granted the power over us mere mortals. After that group, a lot of the rest are Bettys."

She looked around the cafeteria. "Any Archies?"

I had no clue what she was talking about. When I blinked, she explained.

"Archie, Veronica, and Betty. An old comic book I had once."

I shrugged helplessly.

"It doesn't matter," she said with a slim smile. "Some other day."

"Okay," I said. "Can't wait."

She looked at Veronica shimmying back and forth. "I've met her type before," she said with a knowing nod. "What about the Bettys?"

"Smart is the first prerequisite," I explained. "That sort of nullifies you from the Beez right away even if you are somewhat hot. Think of it like finding a hair in your nachos. Smart and hot don't mix together very well in this school. 'Mutually exclusive' if I remember math class correctly."

She laughed. "And the rest?"

"The rest don't really matter," I told her. "No one else has names for everybody but I call them the Gears, Ganjas and Goths. The Gears hang out in near the automotive shop and the Ganjas rule over the second floor bathroom. Room two twenty two, I think. It'll be the smoky one that smells funny. The Goths only get the dark corners."

"Interesting," she said. "No vampires or werewolves?"

"Not lately. I think they hated the cold winters. Blood got so thin they went to the west coast to hang out in the woods and chase pasty white girls. Washington, I think."

"Funny," she said. "Sort of."

"You asked," I said with a shrug. "And, oh yeah, I almost forgot. We do have a few black kids too. Added in like pepper from a shaker. Applied sparingly."

"You a hater?" she asked as she studied me. She was joking as far as I could tell.

"No, not at all," I answered. "Actually I like pepper. Anyways, the black kids mix and match into all of the groups pretty randomly. At the end of the day they get bused back to the city. Most don't live in Greendale. I think it's illegal for them. They might get busted."

A questioning smile crossed her face. "This isn't some northern Klan area is it?"

I shook my head no. "It's pretty white around here, but no one runs around in bed sheets as far as I've seen. Actually, I don't think I even *know* a black kid. How's that for living in a nice little bubble?"

"Safe. Ignorant. Probably both." She slipped open the zipper on her backpack and continued. "So where do you guys fit in?"

I looked at Curt as he scratched a ripening zit on his chin. I was embarrassed to say but decided to tell her the truth. So I looked at her black eyes and spoke.

"We don't," I said. "We're sort of like those annoying flies that buzz up against a closed window. People pretty much ignore you and hope you go away."

"Or you get swatted," she said.

I considered her remark. "Good point."

"Those flies really suck," said Curt as he crushed his wrappers into a small ball. "When I was a kid a neighbor of mine would feed flies to spiders. They'd get eaten alive."

Renee looked at me quizzically. I shrugged again and offered an explanation.

"Never mind Curt. He's had a rough past." He gave me a dirty look but I kept on. "I think maybe the surfboard loosened a screw or two. But he's a dork through and through. Same as me. We're proud to carry the Dorkian flag."

She shook her head side to side. "So I'm sitting next to a couple of flag wavers," she said with fake contempt. Then she added. "Maybe I'll join your little club. It appears two might be a lonely number."

I choked a little. Me? In a club? I thought of some old dead dude who said he wouldn't want to be in any club that would have him. I almost told her that but Curt spoke first.

"A club. How interesting," he said. "I could be treasurer."

"And I'll be keeper of the magic key," I said in a sarcastic voice.

Renee got my drift. "We'll hold off on the club for now. Anything else I should know about you two?"

Curt's tongue flopped out of his mouth at that one. "I'm a four-o student," he offered. "I hope to get a scholarship to Wisconsin someday. Probably go to grad school too."

"Good luck with that," said Renee. "I'm just hoping to get through high school." She paused. "How about you, Jimmy?"

I looked at Curt and knew my two point nine grade point

couldn't match his annoying habit of straight A's. *So where do I start?* I thought. That I was like a lab rat in a cage looking for a way out? That even after one year in high school, I couldn't wait for *anything* different than I already had? The sad fact was I didn't know what I would do next. So I hid my dirty little secret and flipped the question. Then I forged ahead like a blind man in a carnival funhouse.

"Nothing interesting about me," I answered as honestly as I could. "I'm like a crappy TV in a hi-def world." I took another bite of sandwich and plowed ahead. "Enough about my limitations. Where do you think you'll fit in?" I asked. "Even though it's your first day and all."

She looked around the packed lunchroom and the jumped at the sound of the ten-minute warning bell. She flinched and her lips became tight.

"I don't. Square peg, round hole. I like to stay pretty much solo, most of the time," she said. "I seem to do best that way. But I'm glad you guys don't mind if I sit with you. I'm feeling my way around the place." She looked over the lunchroom. "It'll take me a while to get used to it here. It's such a big school."

"Bigger than the ones you've been at?" I asked.

She nodded as she dug deep in her backpack and pulled out an apple. "Way bigger," she replied. "At least twice the size. Newer. It's probably the nicest school I've ever gone to." She took a bite of the apple and looked around again. "It looks like everybody else in here belongs though. You know what I mean, Jimmy?"

I knew exactly what she meant, more than she could imagine. In fact, I never belonged *any* place as long as I could remember. Even in third grade I was the classroom bedwetter who pissed his pants. To this day it was like I was still sitting in pee waiting for everyone to discover my wet secret.

I bit down on my lip but drew back when it stung. "I know what you mean. Unfortunately, that's the way it's been for a long time. Every day I think maybe it'll be different. But different never happens."

She bit into her apple and by accident her elbow touched mine. The tiny zinger appeared again and I pulled away slowly before she spoke. "You're smart, aren't you?"

I didn't know how to respond to that. *Freakin' Einstein only wished he were as smart as me,* I almost said. I considered her question. No one ever told me I was smart before; certainly not my parents or teachers and certainly not a girl in my class.

"I get mostly B's," I answered.

"I don't mean grades," she said. "You're smart in other ways. You think about things. Don't you?"

She was right. I did think about things. All the time to tell the truth. So much that sometimes I thought my brain would split like an overripe melon and the gork from inside would fall out and cover my desk. Renee was the first person to ever notice.

"Ummm," I said as if trying to prove her whole theory wrong. Eventually a few words sputtered out. "I guess I do think about stuff but that doesn't mean I'm smart. In fact, maybe I waste my time on useless random thoughts that are a waste of gray matter."

"That's my point exactly," she said. "Whether they are random thoughts or not, at least you're thinking. That's a lot more than most people do. Most girls I know are more worried about how big their boobs are and most guys just want to catch a feel. They both seem like gigantic wastes of time." She rolled the half-eaten apple in her hand and studied the bruised spots. "So ends the gospel according to Saint Renee."

I tried to ignore her comment because I wasn't opposed to a little hand-hockey with a girl someday. I was caught off guard and at a loss for words. Renee was different from anybody I knew and I had talked to her for a grand total of about fifteen minutes.

"You do seem sort of saintly," I said trying to inject a joke. "Kind of like a young Mother Theresa in Levi's."

"That's a weird thought," said Curt as he reentered the conversation. "I wonder if she would wear them."

"She's dead, douche," I said. "For years now."

"I guess that would make it difficult," he replied.

Renee and I smiled and raised our eyebrows at exactly the same time. A second later I choked on the last piece of my sandwich and thought I was going to need a quick Heimlich. After I coughed a few times the chunk of bread re-surfaced and I caught my breath.

"What?" asked Curt. "She would help sales. I hope to get into marketing someday," he explained as he licked applesauce off his lips.

"I like the angle. I can see you as a marketing genius," said Renee. "Just you wait and see."

"Don't encourage him too much. Or someday he'll be burning in hell for leading pious woman to the fires of damnation on Madison Avenue. Trying to sell 'Mother Theresa's Apple Bottomed Jeans, boot cut optional'." I knew it wasn't that funny but Renee still laughed. A full and deep laugh, not that little "tee-hee" that most girls squeak out when they meet somebody new. A laugh that made you happy just by hearing it.

"See? What did I tell you?" she replied when she settled down. "I told you you're smart. Funny too."

I blushed a little when she said that. I thought I *was* funny even if hardly anyone else did. Half the time Curt didn't get my jokes and I had to be content with amusing myself. At least I finally had someone who would understand my sense of humor.

"I try," I admitted. "I think I'm an acquired taste."

"Like sardines," said Curt. "Please don't encourage him, Renee. He'll never stop. I know from experience."

"I'll be careful," she promised. "I wouldn't want him to get a big head."

It was at that moment a pair of dark shadows appeared over the table. I stiffened and dipped my head in Renee's direction. I turned mute when I saw it was Vance Rithrow, one of the biggest Billys of them all. At his side was Veronica Styles who stood like they were joined at the hip. Vance had on his typical t-shirt two sizes too small to show off arms busting out like boulders from the sleeves. He had copper-colored skin baked on at the tanning salon for moments just like this. When he smiled, a perfect line of white teeth accented his spiked blonde hair. He had bumped into me once or twice in the hallways and I bounced off him like a ping-pong ball. Veronica was closer to perfection than I imagined even in my sloppiest dream. She smelled like coconuts and I had a surge of pure lust done teenage style. I reigned in my hormones as quickly as I could and tried to erase my evil thoughts. I doubted the two of them were here to shoot the bull with me and it didn't take long to find out I was right.

"I'm guessing you're new in school," Vance said as he stood behind Renee and put a meaty hand on her shoulder. I could have sworn he flinched before he spoke. "I don't think I've seen you before. I would have noticed."

Renee didn't move a muscle. "I've been around," she lied without missing a beat. "You just must have ignored me last year."

That stopped Vance for a second and he measured her up. He let go with another brilliant smile before he spoke.

"I don't think so," he said. "I couldn't miss a girl as pretty as you."

"Your plan usually works, doesn't it?" asked Renee.

I had no idea what she meant. Apparently neither did Vance.

"My plan?" he asked.

"The major smile. The flex in the triceps. Nice touch."

He pulled his hand away and looked at Veronica for help. She didn't miss a beat and slid into the seat next to Renee. "We like to welcome the new kids here as soon as we can. We think it's the least we can do. I'm Veronica. Veronica Styles." She turned up the volume on her name as if it was already a legend in her own time. She held out her hand and waited for Renee to reach out.

Between her blazing smile and the smell of coconuts I got dizzier than if I was duct-taped to a tilt-a-whirl. I felt like I should say something, but if I opened my mouth I was afraid I would hurl. So I choked down my partially digested lunch and stayed quiet.

Renee took her hand and Veronica's face tightened. I could have sworn a layer of some expensive powder wafted out of her pores. Then Renee spoke. "Veronica Styles," she repeated. "Most people are charmed, I'm sure. Or intimidated."

As far as I could tell, Veronica took that as a compliment. Just the same she pulled her hand away from Renee.

"So you were here last year?" she asked in a questioning voice. "I must not have seen you."

Renee set her apple core down on the table before she spoke. "I started late," she said. "I was only here the last few weeks."

Veronica nodded in understanding. "Then you'll need a personal guide. I know *everyone* so I'll help you. Just follow my lead."

Renee's lips got tighter before she replied. "I do okay by myself. I don't need anyone to run interference for me. Thanks anyways."

The surprise on Veronica's face was evident and her neck muscles turned hard. I suspected it was new for her to have anyone question her authority. Especially an unknown girl from Whoville.

"I can make life easier for you if you want. Just say the word." She said the last syllable through gritted teeth as if it were more a demand than a request. Renee was having none of it.

"No thank you," she said. "I'm a big girl and I'll figure it out by myself."

Veronica stiffened again and I waited for the inevitable fangs to come out. Right on cue she bared long rows of her own perfect teeth and hissed a reply.

"Not a good idea, new girl. This is my school and you're only a visitor. Remember that and we'll get along just fine. Okay?" Then an air-brushed smile appeared.

Renee almost smirked at the words. "Is that so? If I didn't know better that almost sounds like a threat."

"No, honey. It's just the way it is."

Renee nodded and her eyes narrowed to slits. "FYI girlfriend, I've been around girls a lot badder than you before. Girls so messed up they would jack your Maybelline and give you an enema with it."

Before Veronica could even answer Vance stepped back into the picture.

"Girls, girls," he said. "I'm sure you'll get along just fine." He returned his attention to Renee. "I still have a hard time thinking I didn't see you last year. I keep my eyes open."

Renee nibbled at her apple and turned her attention to Vance. "Well, it's true," she said. "It's probably that this summer I kind of grew into myself. I even got a new hairstyle and everything. Kind of like a teenage makeover sort of thing." She stopped and looked straight at me with those eyes. "Right, Jimmy?"

I was afraid of being drawn into it, couldn't weenie out of it now. *What the hell*, I thought. It wasn't as if things could get a lot worse for me even though Vance could crush my head like a peanut shell and Veronica could get me blackballed so quickly even the AV Club would reject my application.

"Well," I started slowly, "you *were* a bit of a skeez last year. Ratty hair and a face like a piece of bacon. Plus your ass was a lot bigger."

Renee kind of snorted and Vance blinked a few times. Veronica just crinkled her forehead in confusion. I laid it on a little thick, but once I got going the words slid out of my mouth like they were on a slip n' slide. Vance seemed to be having a little more trouble.

"I, uhh …" he said. "I'm sure you weren't that bad." He leaned over and looked at me. "What was your name again?"

"Jimmy," I replied. "Jimmy Parker."

He nodded. "I'm sure Jimmy is exaggerating a bit. No one can change that much over a summer."

"That's for sure," added Veronica. "It's close to impossible to drop a size or two. I should know …"

She stopped talking as if she revealed more than she wanted. I looked at Curt and he shrugged as if he had no freakin' idea what was going on at the moment. I almost did the same before Renee spoke again.

"Well, I did," she said. "Thanks to a new cleanser my face really cleared up. Even better I finally found a shampoo that didn't fry my hair and make me look like a ... a ..."

"Skeez," I said under my breath.

"Yeah," she agreed. "I lost thirty pounds on a grapefruit and corn flakes diet. And I only have a few stretch marks left. Anyways, it's nice to only wear my retainer and scoliosis brace at night now. My back is straighter and my gums hardly bleed at all anymore."

Veronica looked as if she was hypnotized and stared at Renee like she was some foreign animal in the zoo. I bet if she had a peanut she would have tossed it across the table just to see if Renee would scurry over to pick it up.

"I'm guessing you think you're funny," Veronica said. "Well, guess what? You're not."

"Darn. And I was so hoping you'd like me. Now I don't know what I'll do with myself."

Veronica licked her lips and replied. "I have an idea but I can't say it. I'm not that rude."

"Sure, Veronica. Thanks for holding your tongue. I'm sure it's better used for other things anyways." I blew a little milk out of my nose but Renee wasn't quite done yet. "And thanks for coming over. If it's okay with you I would like to finish my lunch now."

Veronica's eyes danced around and she was lost for a response. *Who did this girl think she was?!* her face said without a word leaving her lips. Then she spoke, "It's a long year, new girl. Just watch yourself. Stuff happens around here. More than you can imagine."

Renee didn't blink. "My eyes are wide open. They have been for a long time. thank you both for coming."

Vance acted first and started to stand up. He looked confused and angry at the same time so I dared not say anything.

"Well, we'll go then," he said. "I'm sure I'll see you again, umm—"

"Renee," she interjected. "And you are?"

"Vance. Vance Rithrow."

"Nice to meet you too," she said as he backed away a few steps. "Maybe I'll see you around at the next dance. I'll look for you. Veronica it has been a pleasure to meet you. Maybe we can have a sleepover someday soon. Talk about boys and stuff. "

I both admired and feared Renee at the same time.

"We're not done yet, new girl," Veronica warned. "Not by a long shot."

The oxygen froze in the air as Veronica retreated with Vance. Renee gave a little flip of her wrist as they both recoiled into the distance.

We stayed quiet until they were out of earshot. It was then Renee started into her syrupy laugh again before Curt spoke.

"Just what was that?" he asked. "You guys can't mess with a Billy and a Beez like that. No one does."

"Yes we can!" said Renee in an excited voice. "And what kind of name is Vance? That just sounds stupid."

"Vance wanted a piece of you, Renee, and you blew it," I said. "He could have made your year. I bet you're off Veronica's party list."

She nodded "I'll live just fine without Veronica. I'm not afraid of girls like her. In fact, sometimes I like the fight more than anything." She paused. "And I bet my ass is still too big for Vance. How did you know about that?"

I shrugged and played it nonchalant. "Just a lucky guess. You look a little big-boned so I made a deduction."

"Big-boned *and* fat-assed? Wow! You really know how to sweet talk a girl."

"Ahh, you wouldn't be the first," I bragged as Curt rolled his eyes. "Just another notch in the 'ol bedpost."

"Very impressive, Jimmy," she said as the final bell sounded. "You could be a Billy someday if you wanted."

That one stopped me.

"You're kidding, right?"

She shrugged. "Maybe. Maybe not. But it might be fun to try." She looked toward Veronica and Vance. "What goes up must come down, right?"

"I guess," I replied in a wimpy voice that quivered more than I liked.

"Anyways, thanks for the lunch together. I hope we can do it again," she said as she moved away from the table.

"For sure," I said and half-waved as she disappeared into the masses.

When her view was replaced by one of The Hot Table my shoulders tightened right on cue.

Chapter Two
Spoon Fed

Most of high school was about as thrilling as getting a Slushee brain-freeze. But in my first class after lunch a thin vein of gold appeared within the red bricks of the old building. English Composition was taught by Clarice Weatherspoon, a wrinkly lady that just about everybody called Mrs. Spoon. She was about eighty years old and one of those teachers who probably taught during the depression and was never going to die. I could see her in a coma maybe, but not dead. I never cared much for writing but Mrs. Spoon was supposed to be different. Fun was too strong a word for her class, but at least it wasn't supposed to bore the living crap out of you. She only weighed a hundred pounds carrying a backpack full of Big Macs, but when she spoke she came on as tough as a leather boot. Probably tougher.

"Please find a seat and stop with the chitter-chat," she said when we entered her room. I grabbed a seat toward the window so I could daydream as much as I wanted without serious interruption. Mrs. Spoon had other ideas. "Eyes up front," she said as we settled into our seats.

"This'll suck," whispered a kid from behind. "Writing is such bullshit."

I didn't say a word and twiddled with my mechanical pencil. The usual gangs had formed and fragments of Billys, Beez, Bettys, and Wafers set up house in the four corners of the room. Vance and Victoria sat next to each other and ruled over their pack near the door. I suspected it gave them a better view of the buzz in the hallway during class time. My brain still buzzed on its own and signaled a hell of a lot more than a load of earwax.

Mrs. Spoon sat on the edge of her desk and tapped a pen on the metal rim. She had a mixture of white hair with a few shocks of gray that made her look like Frankenstein's bride. Or maybe even his Grandmother. I think even her wrinkles had wrinkles, but they did nothing to hide the energy that burned from her blue eyes. They were spooky to look at and it was like a juju spell when she stared at you. For that reason and maybe because of her reputation as a general hard-ass everyone settled down quickly.

"Nice to see you all today," she said. "My name is Mrs. Witherspoon but you can call me Mrs. Spoon if you like. In fact, most kids do." She paused and looked over the classroom towards the back row. "I hope I get to know all of you during the year. Even those of you who hope to remain invisible in your seats and disappear from view."

I slumped into my chair as if I had turned into melted cheese. I knew some of the people in the class by name, but had barely spoken to more than three or four of them. Most times my freshman year it was like my lips were super-glued together and for as much as I talked in class I could have been born without vocal cords. I almost never spoke up unless forced and doubted things would change with Mrs. Spoon. When she walked down the middle aisle she had my attention.

"I'd like to introduce a new student to the school," she said as she stopped in front of a desk. I craned my neck and wasn't disappointed. "Class please welcome Renee Wizenson." Mrs. Spoon smiled and held out her hand which Renee took slowly. They looked at each other and I had a crazy feeling they were looking *inside* each other. Mrs. Spoon's juju eyes got a little wider and she quieted for a second until Renee let go. We all waited for her to say something but Renee beat her to it.

"I'll do the best I can," she said as if a question had been asked. "Though it is nice to be welcomed."

Somebody choked out a laugh that was followed by a few more. I guessed they thought Renee was sucking up. Truth be told, so did I.

"I know some of you think writing is bullshit," Mrs. Spoon said and looked in my direction. I almost panicked and told her *I* hadn't said anything but swallowed it back knowing it would be a true geek move. Then she looked over the room. "Depending on what is written, sometimes you might be right. When it is done correctly writing opens the soul and lets our inner being surface. When the unvarnished thoughts each of you possess find their way onto paper they are pure as Wisconsin snow." She stopped for a few seconds as if she was transported a thousand miles away. "It will be that way for some of you. Just you wait and see." She ignored a couple of muffled groans and her eyes narrowed into slits. "I want to see what is inside of each of you. You should want the same of yourself. To examine the life we have been granted."

"That's so heavy," said Veronica. "We'll like have to be intro-septic."

The room was silent for a few seconds then a reply sounded. "I think the word is introspective," corrected Renee.

I knew no one else knew her and I waited for Veronica to explode. I worried about what Renee was getting herself into. Part of me believed she didn't even care.

Veronica turned to face Renee and narrowed her eyes. "Who asked you, new girl?"

"Just trying to be helpful," she replied.

"If I need your help I'll ask for it but you can bet I'll never ask." Veronica gave a little turn of her head as if the case was closed permanently.

Renee nodded but didn't back away. "Fine," she replied. "I'll be here when you need me."

"Girls, stop," said Mrs. Spoon. "My classroom is cordial and no place for acrimony."

Veronica shook her head and replied. "I'm so sure, Mrs. Spoon. What does divorce have to do with it?"

Mrs. Spoon paused and considered her own words. "Acrimony, not alimony. They are different things although they often do go together."

The class laughed, at least the ones that got the joke. Renee just got a glare from Veronica that could have burned off a barbwire tattoo.

"As I was saying," continued Mrs. Spoon. "I will attempt to make you think about your past, present, and future. Then teach you to put what you have discovered onto paper in a coherent manner." She paused and let her words sink in. Then Renee spoke again.

"What if life is so crappy that it shouldn't be put on paper? Maybe it would be better that way. Isn't that a possibility?"

Mrs. Spoon waited to respond. Then instead of saying anything, she nodded her head for a second as if she was considering the truth of the question.

"Possibly," she said. "What I think, Renee, is that the truth unleashed, whether it be good or bad, is always preferable than keeping life bottled up inside. No one can exist with that pressure for very long. Not you, nor me. Writing can release your spirit and ultimately change who and what you are. I truly believe that. As the year goes on, I suspect you will too."

Renee shook her head like she wasn't totally convinced. "I guess we'll find that out, Mrs. Spoon. Time will tell."

"Time is of the essence, isn't it? I'm looking forward to a new year and new thoughts. Be they bland or brilliant, they need to be exposed and illuminated. I believe we will all be the better for it."

A nervous energy vibrated and I slid down further into my chair. Mrs. Spoon slid skinny glasses across the bridge of her nose and picked up a stack of paper from her desk. "My class is easy if you write from the heart and don't avoid the truth as you see it. Remember those words as I give you your first assignment." The groans that followed only seemed to embolden her. "Your assignment is to write your own obituary that reflects on your life up to this point. Be it sports, arts, or whatever. I would also like you to note its impact on society. This is not a morbid assignment. It is an exercise in allowing you to reflect on your accomplishments or lack thereof." The small ripple of groans increased and a few whispers escaped. "We will do it today."

"Are you kidding?" said Veronica from her spot in the room. "Homework on the first day?" Vance nodded his agreement, which set off a few more Beez-lite drones to do the same.

"I'm afraid so," she replied. She smiled like some old witch doctor before she finished. "I will keep them to myself and not share them with anyone else. At the end of the year we will repeat the assignment and compare the two. I think some of you might be quite surprised at how much you have grown. Or hasn't." She paused for effect. "I'll hand out composition paper and you will have half an hour to complete the assignment."

The chairs scraped across the floor and grumbling overtook the classroom. I squirmed and hoped Renee would notice I was there, but she was transfixed on the paper Spoon handed her. When I got mine I curled over my desk to shield it from view. The sound died down and most of the class busied itself with the assignment. I put my head in my hands and closed my eyes for a while and tried to think. Then I started to write:

Dweeb Dies of Severe Boredom

Jimmy Parker of Greendale, Wisconsin, passed away yesterday after succumbing to a lifelong bout of never-ending indifference. Jimmy fought the brave fight but unexpected complications set in after he suffered an acute attack of teenage weariness manifesting itself in brain matter implosion.

Young Jimmy had admittedly not accomplished much during his fifteen years on earth. He was most proud of his achievement of being potty-trained at the age of six and leaves behind a large collection of erasers donated to the kindergarten class at St. Alphonsus School. He took pride in once scoring in a sixth-grade basketball game when he banked in a free throw after being fouled by an especially clumsy opponent. Unfortunately, the point was taken away when the referee determined that his toe was an inch over the line. He was also proud he had made it all the way to "Tenderfoot" in the Boy Scouts of America before quitting after being ridiculed for burning the meal at an overnight campout.

Jimmy is survived by his real estate dealing mother, Dana, and his car salesman father, Tony. Both were unable to be reached but messages were left on their cell phones. Cash memorials should be sent directly to the International House of Pancakes where Jimmy spent the majority of his free time. Given a warm day and a strong breeze, Jimmy's ashes will be scattered over the skateboard park located at Loomis Road and 27th Street. In case of rain well-wishers are advised to stay home and watch a rerun on TV in Jimmy's honor.

So there it was. My testimony to my life and death. I'm not sure it fit Mrs. Spoon's specific intent, but on short notice it was the best I could do. I handed the paper in and my gut turned over. I have a head packed full of sarcasm and realized the obituary might come back to bite me in the ass. When the bell sounded what was done was done.

"Thank you all for your work today," said Spoon from the front of the room. "I believe this year we will have a lot of fun together; whether, at the moment, you believe it or not."

That was met with more grumbling and was quickly overtaken by the screech of chairs on the freshly waxed floor. I stood up and caught Renee's glance just before she made her way through the door. When I followed the pile of bodies I was happy she noticed me.

"Howdy, stranger," she said as a greeting.

"Well, hey there," I said in my best stud voice. "How's my little cupcake?" I waited to see if she would play along and seconds later was not disappointed.

"Soft and fresh." She crinkled her nose. "Wow, that sounds weird doesn't it?"

I shrugged and settled my backpack. "Soft is good. I like fresh."

"I guess," she said helplessly. "I just don't want to lead you on. I have my reputation, you know."

"Umm, no you don't. At least not yet as far as I can tell."

"Pure as sugar, I would say. For now."

"Well, you're safe with me," I said lamely as she brushed up against me.

Hell, she never knew how safe she was. I read somewhere where teenage boys think of sex every seventeen seconds and last year I timed myself to see if it was true. That day I averaged over thirty seconds and I worried there was something wrong with me. I had never even been on a date and probably wouldn't be anytime soon. I think most girls viewed me as their little brother who was cute in a baby-faced way. After I watched a special on the History channel about Dillinger and his gang, I stole a nickname from one crazy guy they talked about. Baby Face Parker, I called myself. Cute *and* dangerous.

"I bet I am safe," she said and surprised me by ruffling the back of my hair. "Mr. Baby-face."

I shivered at the words and drew back.

"Why would you call me that?" I asked.

She shrugged, but didn't look away. "Just because. No other reason."

I was at a loss for words, when she moved closer I kept a space between us. I stiffened and tried to remember the last time I was this close to a girl. It was probably when I slow-danced with a girl named Maggie at an eighth grade mixer. I remember crushing her toes at the same time I developed a little woodie. I'll never forget it because when we got close it was the first time I ever felt a tit. Not with my hand but on my own bony ribcage. The guys in our class nicknamed her "Bodacious" and it wasn't because of her big personality. For all I know she had the mind of a Greek philosopher, I was more concerned with the size of her twin towers. I still have dreams about that girl—even if since then she's gained about a hundred pounds and her chest is now the size of a small watercraft.

"Maybe," I shrugged. "it was weird you called me that." We walked a few feet and I realized for the first time how short she was. The force of her personality made her seem taller but I bet she topped off at just over five feet. "You're shorter than I thought," I blurted out.

She blinked at me and shook her head from side to side. "Okay," she said. "You're skinnier." She paused and I was sure I had pissed her off. "I'm just as tall as I'm supposed to be, don't you think?"

I had no real answer for that. "I just meant you seemed taller sitting down—if that makes any sense," I tried to explain. I shook my head and realized how stupid I sounded. *Dumb ass*, I thought.

"No sense whatsoever but I'll forgive you." She brushed back a strand of hair from her forehead and stepped into the hallway. "What did you think of Mrs. Spoon?"

"Interesting," I replied. "I like her."

"She loves what she does. That's for sure," said Renee. "She's different."

"In a good way, I think." She wasn't a cookie-cutter teacher who treated us like stale leftovers reheated again and again. She looked you in the eyes like she knew something. Actually, maybe that had me just a little bit scared.

"So what did you write?" Renee asked. "Anything good?"

Good question, I thought. Who's to say what was good? I know teachers get paid to grade us but what do they *really* know? It was all in the eye of the beholder as far as I could tell. Who was to say that their eyes were any clearer than mine? Then I blurted out an answer to her question.

"I just wrote down some bullshit. I think it was good. I guess that's what matters."

Renee looked at me with her hands on the straps of her backpack.

"Spoken with conviction just as Mrs. Spoon would want. You're already a convert."

"Like a witless Jehovah's Witness," I said. "So what did you write?"

Before she even had a chance to answer, the moment was broken by a familiar voice.

"You two again?" asked Vance as he stepped forward from the crowd. "You got something going on?" Veronica was at his side and watched intently.

Renee seemed to grow larger in front of my eyes. "Sure do. He's my lover," she said. "He's incredible."

I could feel my face turn red at her words. Her smile seemed to piss off Vance more than she probably intended. The problem was he decided to direct his anger at me. This time I didn't feel as funny as I did in the lunchroom. I remembered Vance almost dismembering a dude on the football field last year after a vicious tackle. He even went gonzo after the tackle like he was human Exhibit A for roid-rage. So I braced for a major impact.

"That right, loverboy?" he asked. "You pretty good in the sack? I think that's pretty freakin' hard to believe."

His words drew the attention of a few junior Billys that were standing behind him. They lined up and I wondered how I had gotten drawn into all the shit in the first place. In a battle of Jimmy versus Billys I was a lamb waiting to be slaughtered by a butcher named Vance.

"I ... uhh," I finally stuttered out.

"I ... uhh, what?" he asked.

"Leave him alone," said Renee. "I was just kidding."

Vance looked at her before he turned back to me. Then he stuck out an index finger and pressed it against my chest. He dug it in deeper and took half a step closer until a vein popped out from the side of his forehead. It was big as a pencil and was purple like an old bruise. But what I cared about most at that moment was the dent he was making in my sternum.

"Lighten up, Vance," I said in a voice that came out terribly close to a whine. "Why don't you just stop?" That only made him press all the harder. I waited for something to give, like my chest bone that was sure as shit going to break like a sheet of ice. Then something strange happened. Maybe it was a reflex, maybe not. Almost on its own my hand shot up to knock his away. Unfortunately, I missed and caught him in the throat with the web of my hand—sort of like a pussy kung-fu move. I gasped more than he did when he fought to draw in a breath. Vance grabbed his throat and backed away with eyes madder than a snake. All he could do was gag as the crowd hooted and hollered. When he caught his breath, I was ready to get the crap beat out of me when a soft hand was placed on my shoulder.

"Is there a problem?" said Mrs. Spoon from behind.

"The little geek hit Vance!" said Veronica. "I saw it!"

So it went in part two of my introduction to Veronica. She had the rep of making or breaking kids and I was teetering squarely on the edge of permanent banishment from the high school society. I looked away from her blue eyes before returning my attention to a more imminent threat. Vance's purple vein was still bulging and he rubbed his throat. He swallowed thickly before he spoke.

"It was an accident, Mrs. Spoon. There's no problem," he said in a voice that came out closer to a croak. "At least not yet."

Renee stepped ahead of me. "We were just talking, Mrs. Spoon. Jimmy was showing Vance a trick. They're actually friends."

Mrs. Spoon cocked her head to the side and didn't seem to be buying the explanation. "Is that true, Jimmy?"

With sweat soaking my armpits, I nodded like a dimwit mule and was relieved I didn't bray like one. "Yeah," I said. "Everything is okay."

Mrs. Spoon exhaled and when the class bell rang she moved aside like a referee at a boxing match. "Then get yourselves moving," she said to everyone. Then she narrowed her eyes. "I better not get wind of anything going on between you two."

"No wind at all, Mrs. Spoon. Not even a breeze. Jimmy and I are buds," Vance said with another smile that backed me up as much as the finger that had been in my chest. "We mess around all the time."

"The best of friends," echoed Renee.

"Then go," said Mrs. Spoon with a slow nod of her head. "Or you'll all be late for the next class."

When I pulled my backpack onto my shoulder, I felt like I was starting to sink in quicksand. In some ways, I already was.

***

The rest of the day was a blur and I stumbled through it like a zombie from hell. I was like a few hundred other students, so I guess I blended right in. Except for the small matter I was waiting for Vance to beat the piss out of me at almost any time. Losers like me just didn't touch a Billy like him. They viewed life from the front row while I had a pair of binoculars and caught a glimpse of the world from the cheap seats. Now, intentional or not, I had put myself directly in the game.

Curt and I walked home from school later that day. I kept one eye peeled for Vance and the other for Renee. I didn't see either and I was kind of grateful. For one, I wasn't looking forward to the beat-down that was going to occur just as sure as the goose crap around Scout Lake. Secondly, as much as Renee brought some excitement into my life, part of me felt like she was a spider drawing me into her web. Like a mysterious black widow direct from Nebraska.

"So you really smacked Vance in the throat?" asked Curt in a high-pitched voice. "I couldn't believe it when I heard it."

I pulled my hoodie up over my head at the mention of his name. It wasn't so much that I wanted to hide as much as I wanted to totally evaporate. Or at least stick my head in the ground like some kind of a freakin' teenage ostrich. There were about a thousand kids storming out of the high school and I imagined I might step on a live grenade any second that would blow me to hell and back.

"Yeah, I whacked him in the throat," I said. "By accident. I should have just taken whatever he was going to give me. I think I had some kind of temporary insanity. Like a short circuit in my hard drive."

"Didn't he kill you?" he asked. "That dude is a gorilla on growth hormones. He's a varsity wrestler too!"

"No shit," I said. "He could gut me like a fish." I stopped and thought of why I did what I did. I still had no clear idea aside from the fact that I might be a moron. No check that. I was a moron. I sighed before I told the truth. "Maybe I just got tired of being me for a minute."

"What does that mean?" he asked.

"Sometimes … some days," I tried to explain. "Don't you ever get pissed that you are who you are and not someone else?"

He shook his head no. "I like who I am."

I hardly knew what to say because that surprised me. I was so far down the high school food chain that I would need a ladder to get up to where the cool freshman protozoa spawned. Even at that I felt superior to Curt. Then it turns out he was happy while I stewed in my own juices like road kill spoiling in the sun. I felt even worse than I did a minute earlier.

"Well good for you," I said. "You should be so happy."

Curt blinked in confusion and followed me as we crossed over the railroad tracks that split the town in half. I looked at a nearby pond and was transported back to a summer day on the shores of Lake Michigan. I was walking on an alewive encrusted beach as the waves pounded away at the flesh-colored sand. I stopped when my chest seized up and leaned over with my hands on my knees to try and draw in some air. Then like a loser my eyes started to tear up and I felt as dead as the dried up fish that lay on the shore. When some people headed my way, I stood up and backtracked away from the water. The sand got whiter the further I moved inland, but I stopped when I saw a black rock about the size of a silver dollar. It was lying half-buried in the sand; shiny like glass but with the rough edges worn away by time. I knelt over, picked it up, rolled it in my palm and wondered how it had gotten into the middle of the abandoned beach. All by itself and as out of place as an altar boy in a strip joint. I brushed off the sand and ran a finger over the smooth surface. I could almost see my reflection on its surface and that made me feel even worse. When the couple holding hands came closer, I slipped the rock into my front pocket and acted like I was cool and bored with the world. Then when I got home, I put my discovery on the nightstand next to my desk. And that's where it is to this day.

"I should be so happy?" Curt repeated what I said a moment earlier. "What is that supposed to mean?"

His voice brought me back and I couldn't subdue my anger.

"You heard what I said." I growled out the words and for a second wondered what was getting into me. I took a breath and looked at the tree-lined streets and wondered how I could feel so shitty in a town as nice as Greendale. When a cloud drifted over the sun it colored the sky a darker shade of grey that just about matched the mood I knew for as long as I could remember.

***

I made it home and tossed my backpack into the back hallway. A voice sounded from a room away and I was surprised my mom was home. I guessed, correctly, she was on her cell phone again. It was to the point that when I thought of her, I pictured her with the thing hanging from her ear like a gigantic earring. When I walked into the kitchen she gave a half-wave and I was sure another big sale was just around the corner. Again. She sold houses for a living and was as addicted to closing the deal as much as a crack addict was to the next hit on a pipe. The market had been down and that made her even more crazed than usual to sell to the next dumb bastard she could talk into it. "Always be closing," she and my dad would joke about a million times as they quoted some lame movie. That never failed to get either of them laughing before they got back on their cells. If I outlive either of them, I'll probably bury them with the damn things on vibrate so they never miss a message.

"Hi Mom," I said in a voice that wouldn't interrupt her. Then I grabbed a bruised banana from the basket and knew I would have to throw a pizza in the oven again.

"It's just the cutest little fixer-upper," she said in a voice so phony I almost spit out a chunk of the freakin' banana. "All it needs is a little TLC."

Join the club, I thought.

She was dressed in some blue suit that probably cost more than she had made in the last few weeks. I noticed the lack of sales didn't stop her from getting her nails done and hair frosted like a bag of powdered sugar was poured on her head. She wouldn't admit to a boob job, but as sick as it is to think of your mom's momba-jambas she sure looked a little top-heavy after she returned from a "short business trip." Weird shit to think about but it is what it is.

Chapter Three
Ring of Fire

I woke up the next day not knowing what to expect. The first day of school I almost got my face crushed and now I was entering round two. *Ding, ding* went a little bell inside my head.

"Are you up yet, Jimmy?" Mom called from a floor below.

I could see it already. By now she had snarfed down half a pot of coffee and checked e-mails on her laptop before I had even opened a crusty eyelid. With her, money was a true love affair of the heart. Money that kept us together in a nice house in the best part of town. Money that kept us apart at the very same time.

"Screw it," I mouthed into my pillow. "I'm up," I shouted in a voice filled with gravel. I rolled over and thought of how much I hated the morning. *The dawn of a new day*, I thought. *New day, my ass,* countered the dark creature that lived in the shadows of my head.

"I have to go," she called into the air. "I'll be back by dinner."

I didn't answer because I knew it was a lie. We hadn't had a family dinner during the week for as long as I could remember. Even Sunday church had been replaced by getting ready for another round of showing houses. Maybe God would understand his place of worship had been replaced by a three bedroom condo with a view.

"Sure, can't wait," I said. I was used to eating by myself; sometimes I even enjoyed the company.

Because it was only about five blocks, I walked to school. Curt usually waited for me a corner or two ahead. I liked the few minutes alone and even with tunes pounding through my earbuds it gave me time to think. Today I alternated between looking out for Vance to avoid getting neutered and thinking about Renee. It was weird about her. She was pretty good looking and all, but I didn't feel *that* way about her. At least I didn't think so. For the most part I am about as horny as the next guy, even though that's a pretty hard thing to measure. It's not like there's a blood test for something like that. Mom would always ask me how my "Mormons" were doing whenever she caught me watching some screwed-up hottie on TV. Of course, that was her way of finding out if my hormones were making me dry hump my pillow like a dog. I'd watch those girls bouncing around with their messed up lives while they chased cool guys and I wondered what it would be like: both being chased and to be a cool guy. But that was fiction I watched through a flat screen or at The Hot Table in the lunchroom. Regardless Renee gave most of those girls on TV a run for their money, but she was different at the same time. Different in a way I couldn't quite figure out yet.

"Just weird," I said under my breath.

"Just weird, what?" asked Curt from a tree he was leaning against.

I yanked out the bud and realized I had spoken out loud. I did that a lot the last few years. I had these conversations in my head as if I was having an argument with my mom or dad or teacher or whoever. Then before I knew it, my lips were moving. It was embarrassing as hell and whenever it happened I pretended I was singing a song or something. More than once I thought I was a freakin' split personality and as crazy as a maggot swimming in horse dooky.

"Nothing," I said louder than needed. Curt was probably the

only guy I could give a little attitude and not get smacked. We met freshman year in cross country and on the first run we randomly paired up together. Since we both sucked, we just started to suck together. He was tall as hell and skinny as a rope and proud of a mustache so dirty it almost blew off in the wind. He had his own smell too—like the inside of my grandma's attic on the third floor. Not really like anything rotting, but a musty smell all the same. Go figure. What really set him apart was he always wore cowboy boots. They weren't the kind that made him look like a rock star, but the pointy-toed kind only a corncob country singer or a complete idiot would wear. Take your pick.

"Sounded like something," he said back. I ignored him and we walked until school came into sight. Then my sigh said it all. "I hear you," he commiserated, "loud and clear."

"Sometimes I wish I could just walk on by," I said. "And avoid the day altogether."

"I hate getting up," he admitted. "Although once I get going I'm okay. I think of the positive things. Like the Robotics Club or something like that."

I almost didn't know what to say. He was so far into geekdom that even if he was thrown a rope he wouldn't grab it. He would probably ignore it and keep on constructing a battery-powered Lego robot that could pick up dog shit and water the grass at the same time.

"You're going to go far, Curt," I admitted with a shake of my head. "No doubt about it."

He looked at me to judge if I was kidding or not. When he realized I was serious he said a strange thing.

"We'll both do well, Jimmy. I can tell." Then he smoothed his fuzzy mustache. "It ain't about right now. It's about where we'll end up."

I was speechless again. I just nodded in agreement until I worked out the answer.

"You may be right, Curt. Unfortunately we're stuck in the shitter right now. For better or worse."

We quieted and tried to blend in with the rest of the kids. Funny thing was I never blended well. Maybe I had a force field around me that kept most kids away. Either that or I had a massive case of BO that did the trick instead. Whatever.

We went in the main entrance and the maze of halls was filled with mice of all sizes. Big, little, tall, skinny—the drill was the same each day. I became jumpy just walking in the place. I didn't need any double chocolate frappaccino cappuccino percolating in my blood to get me jacked up. Just drop me in the middle of about a thousand nameless faces and I was as amped as if I mainlined a thirty-two ounce Mountain Dew.

"See ya," said Curt as he veered off and disappeared into his own little world.

"Yeah," I grunted and headed to my locker to unload crap and figure out my next destination. "It just keeps on getting better," I said a minute later when I checked my schedule and dragged myself to gym class.

***

I suppose there is nothing specifically wrong with the idea of gym. Staying in shape, exercise, screwing around, blah, blah, and blah. When you suck at most physical activity it's no fun getting the fact stuffed in your face. I made my way to the locker room and stopped when I got to my locker. I froze in place and looked at what lay dead ahead. Jammed into the little vents of my locker was a wet tampon that marked I was a pussy for all the world to see. I tugged at the string and flung the waterlogged piece into the corner. It was a message from the Billys and the short hairs on the back of my neck stood at attention. I started to shake, but held my ground until the moment passed. When I gathered enough strength, I slipped shorts on my hairless legs and waited to be humiliated by a gang of Billys that probably started shaving in fifth grade.

Our teacher was Mr. Tindero—a six-foot three, ex-Marine, buzz cut-wearing mass of walking beef that could pop my cranium like a juicy pimple. He liked to be called "Tin Man" and had a reputation of not taking shit from anyone and that included the Billys and Beez. In fact, he was known to give them *more* crap than everyone else. He was kind of thought to be a protector of weak tits like me. Sort of like a Guardian Angel of the Wimps.

"Line up," he said to the pile of us who were already in the gym. We knew better than to question him and the voices quieted quickly. He gave us the usual introduction before telling us what was ahead. "It's a nice day, so we'll meet at the softball field. Jogging all the way."

The groans started even before he got the words out of his mouth. I didn't care we had to run a few hundred yards toward the field. Aside from bowling, I found that it was about the only sporty thing I *could* do. So I took off and trotted toward the baseball diamond and waited at the backstop for everyone else to get there. I knew some of the kids by name but didn't say a word. Until I saw a straggler at the back of the pack.

"Renee," I said with a sort of semi wave of my hand. I hadn't noticed her yesterday morning, but of course we hadn't met yet. She slid through the group and faced up.

"I didn't know you were in this class," she said and nodded towards the others. "Fat chance we have two classes together. The old lady in the afternoon and Captain America in the morning. Brains and brawn." She stepped back and measured me up. "Nice legs. Makes me hungry for linguini."

I swallowed hard at that one. Then I realized she was just giving me crap—in a good way. "I'm working on my tree-trunks," I replied. "That and my rock-hard abs. Thinking of moving to Jersey."

"You're such a Billy wannabe."

"A guy's got to have a dream."

"I'm telling you. It's one that can come true. You just need an in."

"An in to what?"

"To be a Billy just like I said. To get in the inner sanctum and see how the dark side lives. The evil empire and all that shit!"

"That's crazy," I said.

"Maybe. But at least you'll be living on the edge."

"If I live to tell about it, you mean." I paused for a second and had an idea. "Why don't you hang with Veronica if you want to live dangerously?"

She shook her head. "I don't think I have the same credit rating as the Beez. Anyways I already stepped on her painted toenails one time too many already."

"Maybe. But what would I have to offer the Billys? A piece of gum? A place for their fists to land?"

"You have a lot more than that to offer. You just have to dig deep."

"Right," I said and hoped for the subject to change.

She looked at me and her lips got tight. Then the tiniest of lines crossed her forehead before she spoke.

"Lately I've been thinking if we don't take a chance on something what's the point? To survive another day like goldfish in a bowl? Be satisfied with whatever nasty flakes get dropped in our mouths?" Then she shook her head slowly and touched my arm. "Never mind. I'm just talking."

I stood there as a breeze blew through my hair. Renee was becoming one hard girl to figure out. She seemed to listen to what I said and why I said it. It was as if I had a real face around her. That I was more than just a skinny geek that just … well, just *existed.* Like I mattered for the first time in as long as I could remember. The air of the morning suddenly seemed thicker. I ignored it and tried to reply as best I could. "I don't mind talking." I told her. "It's just the words that worry me."

"I don't get it," she admitted as she squeezed my arm harder.

I flinched, but didn't pull away. I was starting to get the feeling she was one of those people that liked to invade your space. It was weird but with her I didn't really seem to mind.

"I could never be a Billy. Never," I repeated.

"We can't just live our life existing, Jimmy. Sometimes you have to take a chance."

I felt like I had been stung and pulled away from her fingers. I swallowed hard and couldn't get a word out right away. *What the hell?* I thought as my mind spun in circles. *Again?* But I was afraid to say anything about it. At least yet.

"So what about what I said?" she asked. "About being a Billy."

I tried to lighten things up and avoid thinking deep. "Not a chance. I couldn't even afford the dues."

"And they are?"

I went yard with that one. "Twenty bucks a month in beer money and ten bucks in gas for the four wheelers. Stogies on demand for the upperclassman and breath mints for the Beez of the day. Vance also gets a ride to school from any newbie Billy he chooses. If they don't he'll bounce them from the club. Then they'll be termites just like the rest of us."

She scrunched up her face and considered my words. "Is there really such a thing?" she asked. "Beez of the day?"

I bluffed. "There sure is. You just have to go online and vote before the school day starts." I nodded with as smug a look I could deliver. "I'll hook you up sister. Stick with me and I'll get you so tight with the major Beez that you'll be able to smell the Chanel they are wearing. When I do, you'll owe me Starbucks for a year. I can taste it already."

She looked at me with narrowed eyes. "I'm not sure if you believe the shit you shovel or not." When she smiled it didn't matter.

***

I got through gym class and hit a single or something, but I didn't really care. Mostly I watched from right field as the usual suspects ruled the day. The Billys rolled their sleeves up as usual so their biceps could impress a whole slew of Beez and Beez in

44

training bras. Veronica was front and center and led the parade of skin on display. She and her shadows wore clothes that would fit middle schoolers and showed off their bags of goodies. "Nothing left for the imagination," my mom's voice echoed in my head. I never told her I imagined way beyond what I saw, so that wasn't the problem. Their bodies drove home the point they were all in a totally different league than I was. I was a scrub compared to major leaguers like them but I told myself I would have my day. Deep down I wasn't so sure.

Renee was actually pretty damn good at softball. She was on my team and hit two doubles and a single. Turns out she was fast too. The second time she scored I high-fived her when she sat down next to me on the bench.

"You're really a good player," I told her. "You must have played before."

"Sort of," she explained. "I played a lot of stickball in San Diego."

"Stickball?"

"We lived in the crappy part of town. The *barrio* the Spanish kids called it. We played in the streets with broomsticks and whatever ball we could find. Sometimes a ball made of string and masking tape. I was good at it and used to play all day."

"I can tell. You're way better than most of the girls."

A familiar voice interrupted. "Most *real* girls don't want to do sports. It's way too butch."

Renee looked at me but my tongue swelled up and tied itself in a square knot. So she turned and replied calmly.

"Butch, Veronica? Really? Maybe you ought to try it before you criticize it."

Veronica stepped back and considered what she had heard. I had to admit I was caught off guard too.

"That's gross and too sick to even think about," Veronica finally said.

"You shouldn't work so hard to hide who you are. Open up the closet a little."

"Whatever. But maybe you should close yours. Literally." She eyed Renee closely. "Your clothes are so ... so *barren*."

Renee didn't skip a beat. "White t-shirts are all the rage in New York. Haven't you seen the new *Glamour*? Mine came yesterday. You better get with it, girl."

I nearly choked and waited for Veronica to attack but she looked confused and turned away. I chalked up another winning volley for the newcomer.

"Game, set, match," I said. "That was crazy." I took a deep breath and settled myself. "You really know fashion?"

"No, dolt. I'm just messing with her. And I'm not a lezzy just in case you were wondering."

"So you just like poking their beehive with a stick?"

She shrugged. "What's she gonna do? Steal the waterproof mascara that I don't have?"

I watched Veronica exit toward more friendly cover. "I guess you're right. I'm just not used to the battles. I'm sort of a behind the scenes kind of guy."

"Then it's time to get in the game, Jimmy. Don't you think?"

"Maybe. But it's safer on the bench." I shook my head in amazement as to how far off track we had gotten. "Games. Softball. Weren't we talking about softball?"

She smiled. "I think we were." Then she turned as bright as I had ever seen. "Mr. Tindel said I play really well. He coaches the girls' softball team in the spring and said I should try out."

"Will you?"

She shrugged but I could tell she was flattered by his thoughts. "Who knows? I might." She paused. "I don't even have a glove though."

"You can have mine," I offered. "It's gathering dust in my bedroom. I sucked in little league. A permanent right fielder if you know what I mean."

"That bad?"

"Worse. I used to hate playing so much I got the shakes like I was having an epileptic fit. Luckily, I quit before I keeled over on the field and woke up with a wallet jammed between my teeth."

"Nice. Well, you only half-suck now if it's any consolation. I'd probably put you in left field on a good day."

"You ought to be a motivational speaker. Right now I'm totally stoked."

"I'll keep that in mind," she said as we walked back out to the field.

When we split up she ran to third base like she had been playing there for years. Then she clapped her hands and shouted encouragement to people she hardly even knew. At that moment I was proud to call her my friend.

***

When gym was over I changed quickly and made my way out of the locker room. I was doing my best to mind my own business, but my backpack had other ideas. I hadn't quite closed it when I shifted it to my shoulder, the zipper slipped and a book dropped to the floor. I reached to gather it in but was blocked by a big pair of Nikes. I was screwed the moment a collection of footsteps left the locker room and stopped next to me. I grabbed the book, but the day just took a serious wrong turn. Like a freakin' head-on collision.

"Hey, tough guy," said some cro-magnum casting a shadow on me. "Vance has been looking for you. He said you're pretty good at cheap shots."

I looked up at a mushroom cloud of blond frizz that belonged to a manimal named Rex. He was as nasty as they came and had broken more bones in football games than a pissed off Incredible Hulk. Rumor had it he once held his hand over a candle flame just to see what burning skin smelled like. It wasn't that he was huge because he wasn't. He was maybe an inch or two bigger than me and until last year I had to stand on tiptoes to pee in the toilet. He had arms coiled like copperheads that rippled when he moved. When his wild eyes focused, my sphincter itself shuddered in fear. That was even before the rest of his friends came from behind and surrounded me. They smiled in a half-assed way and my petrified expression told them all they needed to know. Even worse, I started to stutter like a freakin'moron. I sounded like a full-fledged idiot that had spent about a dozen years *hoping* he would be smart enough for a ride on the short bus.

"Buh, buh, buh," I said as my brain overloaded. When I was little I spent years in speech class and for the most part had the stuttering under control. Now like a rat from a sewer it crawled out just in time for a new school year.

"What was that?" asked Rex. "Buh, buh, buh? Wait until I tell Vance he got popped by a stuttering clown!"

"Vah, vah, vah," I said trying to say Vance's name. I was losing traction and when three Billys closed in it was going to get only worse. A few seconds later I wasn't disappointed.

"Why don't you just leave him alone," said a voice. "I'm guessing Vance can take care of things himself if he wants to. He doesn't need tools like you to do his work."

They turned and faced Renee with a look of amazement. I was sure they had no idea who she was and they all waited for Rex.

"Who the hell are you?" he asked as his tattooed arms rippled. "What do you have to do with anything?"

"First off, I'm no one that you should care about," she said as she looked up at him. "Second, I don't have anything to do with anything. It's just that I hate bullies. Especially ones with fuzz-heads."

"What did you say?"

"You heard me."

He looked too amazed to laugh. Then he reached out and placed his hand on the top of her head like she was a little girl. This only made Renee smile.

"Listen, tiny. I do what I want when I want. You got that?"

She nodded. As he held his pose her eyes brightened.

"Attaboy. Show 'em all what you got," she said. "'Cause you know it's just that, isn't it? A big show."

He pulled his hand back and looked wounded. Only I had no idea why.

By this time the whole group of kids had already started hooting and hollering. The scene drew the attention of Mr. Tindero and he dropped a bag of baseball bats onto the floor. His eyes narrowed to a squint and his eyebrows turned into a mean uni-brow. He smelled the tension and rose up to full height.

"Issues here, boys and girls?" he asked. "Anything I can help with?"

Rex had recovered and flashed a chipped-tooth grin that he kept as a badge of honor from a past game. "Not at all, Tin Man. We were just getting acquainted. Me and my new friends. It's early in the year you know."

He nodded and matched Rex's smile with one that said the kid was a real douche. "Get acquainted some other day," he said. "Right now just get to your next class."

Everyone knew not to mess with Tin Man and today was no exception. The hallway cleared and Rex's glare nearly scorched the peach fuzz on my chin. I walked away with Renee a step behind and didn't slow down until I hit the stairwell. Then I stopped and blurted out exactly what I felt.

"Don't ever do that again," I said looking her in the eye. "I don't need anyone to help me. If I get myself into shit, I'll get myself out of it. I may look like a pussy. I might even be one. But that's my problem. Okay?"

She measured me like a bug under a microscope. She hitched up her backpack over a shoulder and was speechless for the first time since we met. Then the tiniest of smiles creased her lips. "Okay, Jimmy."

I can't say for sure, but I think she was proud of me. Imagine that.

***

I ran my ass off that day in cross-country. Even the coach didn't know what got into me. Mr. Heckbard had coached for about ten years and knew the ropes of running inside and out. What he didn't know was how fast a guy could run when he was all jacked up inside. Between being on the Billys hit list and semi-pissed off at Renee, I ran like a stinkin' madman. I was usually in the second pack of runners securely hidden away from the lead but that day I didn't give a damn. Coach Heckbard sent us on an eight-mile run in the park and wanted us to work it hard. And work it is what I did from the very get-go, I decided to abandon my usual safe spot and take off like a banshee straight from hell. The varsity guys let me go because they had seen a hundred losers start too fast only to die later. But this time they were wrong. I had the adrenaline cranked and I ran until I could hardly see the rest of the team behind me. When I finally hit the school in front of all the others, Coach Heckbard was there to meet me at the door.

"Where is everybody else?" he asked with a wrinkled brow. "Did they take a wrong turn?"

He wasn't trying to make fun of me and given my past performances it was a legitimate question. So I answered him as straight up as I could.

"They're behind me. They'll be in soon."

He still didn't get it and tried again. "Did you cut the course? You won't get any better taking short cuts, you know."

When he accused me of cheating, I was too surprised to say anything. Instead my shoulders drooped when a group of runners entered into view.

"I'll try and remember that next time," I said as the fatigue of the day settled in. Then for whatever reason, I didn't say another word. I guess I was just too tired to fight for myself. Right about then, I was as whipped as a hound dog that could never quite catch what he was chasing. A chase that sometimes wore me out more than anyone would ever know.

Chapter Four
Slow Bleed

I barely woke up in time for school the next day. My mom's voice hollered for me to get up, but by then I only had about fifteen minutes to get there. I jumped in the shower and bolted from the house about fifty seconds later. My hair corkscrewed in three directions and just about matched my brain. I was stuck with gym class again and I prepared myself for another bloodsucking day. I hated getting changed twice before hardly even wiping the gunk out of my eyes, but I had no choice.

I threw on my gym clothes and hoped the collection of Billys would leave me alone. Christ, in two days I had gone from the Invisible Teenager to being on the Top Ten Most Wanted Wimp List. Luckily, they were already in the gym and I just beat the late bell before Tin Man would make me do push-ups. I took a second to catch my breath and walked over to where Renee was standing. She was about five feet behind the rest of the class staring intently at the floor as if she was hypnotized or something. I tried to think of something jazzy to say but fell short.

"Morning," I said in a squeaky voice, "I barely made it on time. Lucky for me or Tin Man would have my ass."

She didn't say a word. It was almost like she was rusted and it took a few seconds for her head to rise up. She looked at me as my shadow covered half her face. For a second it seemed like she hardly knew me. I blinked and felt as if I hardly knew *her.* Her hair was matted on one side and made mine look like I just left some fruity Hollywood stylist. The smile I had come to expect was nowhere to be found.

"Yeah," she said in a flat voice.

That was it. No more, no less. I kind of shook my head as if to clear myself, but realized that was all I was going to get.

"Okay, then," I said and followed the class out the door.

We were playing softball again and I readied myself to take the usual lumps and bumps that were sure to come my way. When I walked next to Renee it was like she was a thousand miles away. I was kind of pissed, because less than twenty-four hours ago we were on the fringe of a solid friendship. Now all of a sudden it was like a leftover in the back of the refrigerator collecting mold. To tell the truth, I didn't find the thought overly appealing. At first I thought maybe she was ticked at me from what I said the day before, but it was different than that. It was Renee that was different. She was in the same body, but was someone I had never met before. It was like meeting a freaky twin and I had no idea what to say to make it right. So I didn't say anything and tried to survive the hour the same way I had done forever. I kept a distance from her and got through the class with a few insults from the Billys, but overall was semi-invisible again. If you got named valedictorian for being inconsequential, I was sure I would be a shoe-in at graduation. When the bell rang I jogged in to beat the rush. Maybe I ran because I was afraid of getting into it with the Billys. The other part of me wanted to keep a little distance from my newest friend.

***

I didn't see Renee at lunch that day. I sat next to Curt and chewed on a salami and cheese sandwich even dryer than usual. I wondered about her but didn't say a word to Curt. I assumed

53

she was one more person who touched my life for an instant but decided she didn't like the way it felt. Then in Mrs. Spoon's class I found out I was wrong.

"What's up, J-man?" Renee asked as she passed me by between two rows of desks. "Ready to rule the world yet?"

I didn't know what to say. Her hair was combed and she gave me the smile that caught my attention in the first place. I almost stuttered but swallowed hard first.

"Nothin' much, I guess," I said in a voice that tried to leash in my confusion. "I wondered if you were going to come to class though." I stopped short and measured my thoughts before deciding to jump into the great unknown. "I thought you were mad at me this morning in gym class. You were … different. Is everything okay?"

Her eyes flickered like fireflies.

"I … I …" she said as she stuttered out her own response. "I wasn't myself this morning. Sorry about that. Someday I'll explain."

I shrugged. It wasn't like I was her teenage shrink. Still, I felt connected to her since the moment she hammered on Vance and Veronica the first day of school. As suicidal as that was for being named Homecoming King and Queen someday, the cheap rush of taking on the best in the school felt awesome. Renee didn't need to apologize for anything in the first place. We were just classmates after all, nothing more and nothing less. So I just stored it away when Mrs. Spoon spoke up from the front of the classroom.

"Settle down, everyone," she said. "I know your excitement is the result of being in your favorite class of the day. Somehow you'll just have to contain yourself." Most of the class groaned, but I liked the old lady. There wasn't any crap she hadn't seen before and that made me feel safe. Just like a boy in a plastic bubble, I sat in my climate-controlled environment, and that was a damn good feeling. Now after only a few days, Mrs. Spoon was stepping to front and center in my "Adults Who Don't Totally Suck" list.

"We'll do our best," said Veronica Styles from a seat near the door. "After all, it *is* the best class of the day."

The sarcasm dripped off her voice and with gum smacking to emphasize she literally absorbed the attention she needed. Vance was sitting right beside her and they high-fived while giving me a cold glare. He hadn't forgotten our confrontation and my day of reckoning would come soon. But in this classroom I was safely wrapped in a roll of double-ply toilet paper.

"Thanks," said Mrs. Spoon. She had it under control and some Victoria Secret never-would-be wasn't going to rattle her cage.

"You're welcome," said Veronica.

"Now it's time to work," said Mrs. Spoon. "I read all of your obituaries and have to admit they were both creative and informative. Some sad and some humorous. They gave me a taste of your personalities, perspectives, and writing ability, or lack thereof," she said with a sigh. "After today's lesson, I will ask you to write a 'flash' assignment that comes from the heart. The only organ in your body that is free from the garbage that rules much of our lives." She waited for the class to stop whispering. "Garbage that we are going to work on getting rid of. Think of this class as a sewage dump for the mind."

"Heavy," said Veronica.

"Let her talk," interrupted Renee.

Veronica glared at her from her seat. "Who asked you, new girl?"

Holy crap, I thought. I wished I could make Renee stop, but it was too late to rein her in. Mrs. Spoon didn't say a word and waited patiently. Almost as if she wanted to see how the confrontation played out.

"Sorry Betty," said Renee.

"It's Veronica."

"My mistake. Good luck with Archie."

Again with the freakin' Archie! I thought. Mrs. Spoon smiled and stretched out a wrinkle.

"What?" asked Veronica as she studied Renee through mascara-drenched eyes.

"It's not important," replied Renee. "Meet you at the malt shop later."

With that Mrs. Spoon decided to end it.

"Enough," she said with emphasis. Then a little smile still curled at her lips.

For now, Renee and Veronica's mini chickie-fight was over. When Veronica tapped a girl in front of her and whispered a few words, I worried that Renee was wandering deeper into a dark world she had no control over. I thought of the whole crew of the Beez as a collection of Stormtroopers right out of Star Wars only instead of white helmets and facemasks they were protected by Christian Dior flesh-colored face paint.

"I think you will all like this class," said Spoon. "Be it heavy or not. All I ask is that you be you." She looked over at Veronica. "Better yet, I'll encourage you to write as you. For some of you that will be quite a change."

"What is that supposed to mean?" asked Veronica. "To write as you? Is that like a riddle or something?"

Mrs. Spoon stopped talking and measured Veronica as a target. I half expected her to rear back and fire a pencil ninja-style through her forehead. Instead she responded slowly.

"Class? Any thoughts?"

I sat and looked at Veronica. She was at the top of her game before she had even reached sixteen years old. I wondered if she would ever fall from her perch and become mortal again. At that moment I didn't have the guts to say anything. Neither did anyone else in the class. Except for one person.

"I'll help, Veronica," said Renee. "Writing is honest if it's done right. That's really all she is asking for."

Veronica sat up straight and took control of the room. Probably for about the thousandth time since she discovered that blond hair and good teeth ruled the world. "You again?" she asked.

Renee sighed. "I didn't think anyone else was going to speak up so I did. I guessed that's why I have a mouth."

"Keeping it shut is also an option. I suggest you try it."

"Her name is Renee," I blurted out. "She can speak if she wants." I almost shit myself when the words busted from my mouth without warning. When my face heated I slinked down in my chair an inch or two.

"And your name is …?" Mrs. Spoon asked.

The world spun a little faster and I took a breath to slow my heart. Then I answered in half the volume.

"Jimmy. Jimmy Parker."

"Thank you, Jimmy," said Mrs. Spoon. I got a staredown from the Billys and Beez and wished for cover that wasn't there. "He is right. My classroom is a place we can speak up freely. Whether we are new to the school or old as dirt like me."

"Or geeks," whispered Veronica under her breath.

"Veronica, something for the class?" Mrs. Spoon asked.

Her gum smacked in rhythm with the shake of her head.

"No, Mrs. Spoon, I'm done."

"Just as I thought," she replied.

But she missed Veronica's darkened eyes that split time between Renee and me.

The class quieted and most kids listened when Mrs. Spoon walked to the front of the room. She was unmistakably in charge and for the moment, no one challenged her, even Veronica. So I listened to her talk about sentence structure and thoughts and how they could be blended like a fruit smoothie and poured onto a printed page. I tried to ignore the intimidating heat of the high school A-List and focused as best I could on the moment. Once the immediate threat faded I started to sweat over the schoolwork that lay dead ahead. Then I shook my head at Renee when Spoon described the assignment of the day.

"In the last ten minutes of today's class, I would like you to tell me what you see for yourself ten years from this date. Not what might happen considering the current economic state of your family, but what you dream in the dream of your dreams. Let yourself go." She paused and brushed back her salt and pepper hair. "Please trust yourself, even though some of you do not."

That was me. I was an expert at keeping thoughts in my head like lit firecrackers ready to blow my brain to Mars. She wanted that out? *Ready or not, Spoonie,* I thought. *Mind diarrhea ready to explode.* So I wrote:

The Future's So Bright, I Gotta Wear Shades

Ten years. Seems like a lifetime. Where will I be? What will I be doing? Seems like a pointless question because I can't even figure out ten minutes from now. That means I have no idea whatsoever but I will make a guess. I would hope by then I would be out of college and working. Working at what, you ask? Don't know, I answer. What do you like, you ask? Not much, I say. But in the slim hope of passing this course, I will try my best to answer the question.

I like dogs, but I hate dog shit, so I guess being a veterinarian is out. I like reading comic books, but I hate writing real stuff (no offense), so I guess being an author is out. I like computers but only if I'm playing video games, so I guess being a computer geek is out. The only other thing that I like is kids, so maybe I can work with them. Becoming a kid doctor takes more brains than I'm supplied with, so that's not going to happen. Maybe I could be a grade school teacher, if that's not too faggy of a thing to be for a guy. Kids need someone to look after them. And I don't ever think I would forget what they need. They need someone to tell them they are important, even if they are imperfect. In fact, it is their imperfections that make them who they are. That they are okay. No matter what.

That was it. I handed it in just as the bell rang and felt dizzy from the effort. I was a better daydreamer than deep thinker and

Mrs. Spoon forced me to think two days in a row! I had a full-on headache after I left her class - a drumbeat pounding in my right temple that hit me harder than a whomp upside the head. Actually, headache and all, it was fun in a painful sort of way. At least it seemed as if she cared about what I had to say.

For a moment I almost forgot that Vance was in the class with me. That was until he elbowed me from the side and sent me flying into the doorjamb. The impact knocked the breath out of me and I almost doubled over, but caught myself just in time. The look on my face made him laugh. Apparently my pain was a pretty funny thing.

"Watch where you are going, Jimmy," he said with a flash of thousand dollar teeth. "I wouldn't want to accidently hurt you."

I swallowed the sting. Vance's friends were having a good laugh and I reached for a good comeback. I was pissed off and scared at the same time. Both emotions courtesy of some squishy organ in my brain I had learned about in science class. So I plowed ahead and did a verbal tap dance.

"It's my fault," I said. "My shoulders got in the way of the door. I've been working big-time on my delts at home."

That kind of shut him up. By the way he looked at me I guessed he wasn't ready for a smart-ass remark.

"You're a weird kid, aren't you?" he asked.

Even though I knew it was a rhetorical question, I answered anyway. "It's all relative," I replied. "I'm just trying to avoid getting the shit beat out of me."

"Oh, it'll happen someday. Believe it," he said.

"I don't doubt that," I said. "But, be careful or you'll get blood all over your nice shirt."

He paused to study me. "I have more of them," he finally said to the amusement of his friends.

I had no real comeback so I just shrugged. I accepted he was probably right about me being weird. I was a little left of center as far back as I could remember. I walked forward and braced for another impact from his elbow or fist but he just shook his head and let me pass. Once again I had escaped. Just like a freakin' high school Houdini with less than nine lives left.

***

That night I sat in my room doing homework and listening to music. The garage door opened and my blood beat a little faster. It had gotten to the point that I both liked and hated being alone. I liked the quiet but dreaded being by myself. Quite a dichotomy Mrs. Spoon might say. Against all likelihood, every day I still hoped life would get better. That thought burned like a tiny pilot light deep inside that was lately running on only thin fumes.

"Jimmy," my father's voice called. "Come down for dinner."

Wow, I thought. Dinner. What a concept. For once I didn't question it and slid a book off of my lap.

"Be right there," I shouted, and so I went.

The kitchen table was filled with white cartons. My dad opened them and set out two plates. The light shined on his bald spot and I wondered if the thinning would spread to me like an infection.

"Got a whole lot of Chinese food," he said with a smug look. "Enough to slant your eyeballs."

"Eyelids," I corrected.

"Huh?" he said as he opened the largest container.

"Eyelids," I said again. "You can't slant eyeballs."

"You know what I meant," he said as the satisfied look fell from his face.

I was sorry I said anything, because the mood blackened. It wasn't often my dad was home for dinner so I should have been grateful for the company. Over the last few years, I drifted away from him like a balloon in the wind. He had never done anything specifically wrong. The problem was he did a whole lot closer to nothing. I felt like an old beat-up car on his lot that had no freakin' chance in hell of ever being sold so it just sat in the back row. "No commercial potential," he would complain to my mom about the beater cars that took up space. I bet if he noticed any rust on my ears, he would say the same damn thing about me.

"Anything new today?" he asked.

I thought about Renee and how Vance got up in my face again after Spoon's class. As I scooped out some white rice, I answered.

"No, not a thing."

He nodded and wiped a drop of soy sauce from his chin. He seemed relieved when his cell phone kicked out a ring tone from his hip. Some half-assed Bon Jovi song about Living on a Prayer or something.

"Tony here," he said a second later. When he liked what he heard, his faced almost glowed. "They want to buy one of those old Cavaliers? I'll be damned!" He looked as if he had died and gone to heaven as he stood and left the table.

I chewed my rice without a sound.

Chapter Five
A Strange Voice

I walked to school and didn't tell Curt about the dream I had the last few nights. It was too weird, both for him and me. For three nights in a row I woke up coughing and gagging like a hard-core bulimic. The dream was pretty freakin' sick. I would get a stomachache and start feeling a little rumble in my gut. Then the rumble turned into a full-fledged psycho merry-go-round. Next I'd get into hacking and spew all over my chest. Then from above, I'd watch as a whole golf ball-sized pile of tapeworms wriggled in a desperate attempt to escape.

I had no idea where the dream came from. Maybe from one of those reality shows where people ate slimy bugs just to win some green. Or maybe from something I learned in biology class when we slit open a few defenseless night crawlers and counted their dead hearts. I almost thought of looking online for a dream-analysis website but was afraid they would say I needed a teenage lobotomy. Any way you sliced it, it was disgusting as hell and I tried to ignore it. And hoped it wouldn't happen again.

"You don't look so good," he said as he sized me up.

I nodded because he was more than right.

"Must have been something I ate," I replied. That was all he needed to know.

***

I bumped through school that day and sidestepped any obvious nukes. I avoided the Killer B's, as Renee called the Beez and Billys, even though they marched through the school like teenage Nazis in black Doc Martens. Today I pulled a disappearing act like a cross-dressing Anne Frank and avoided everything. When school ended, I stretched out for our first cross-country meet of the season and tried to leave the past few days behind.

"You ready to run?" Curt asked.

"Like a man among little boys," I promised. "I plan on kicking butt and taking names." I paused for effect. "I'm sorry sonny, what was your name again?"

"Funny. Let's just hope you can carry your big head around the course without falling over. I plan on whipping your skinny white ass today."

My eyes widened. "You? John Wayne's illegitimate son who wears boots so gay it's like your butthole has a target on it?"

"Leave my boots out of it. When we run, we're in battle and I aim to win."

"Okay, studly, I'll be looking for you out there. If you beat me just shoot me in the head."

"That's a promise, my friend. It'll be an honor."

I smiled at him and felt good. We trash-talked all the time and in some ways that was the best thing about being on the team. I liked running okay, but mostly I liked being part of something. Actually part of *anything* was closer to the truth. When the start of the race neared I needed to psych up even more.

"I'm going to jog by myself," I told Curt.

"Suit yourself," he said tugging at the strings of his spikes.

I stood up and shook out my arms to release the tension setting in. Then I ducked out behind the tennis courts to do a little loop around some old zebra-skinned birch trees. It was there Renee was sitting against the smallest birch with her closed eyes raised to the sun. I veered off to surprise her from behind and slowed my pace to a walk. I was more surprised by her voice as she sang softly to herself. I stopped and listened to the gentle pat of her right hand as she kept a simple rhythm. I didn't interrupt when she blended in with the soft breeze of the day:

Didn't want to go, but I didn't have a choice
Miles on a highway, never had a voice
Another brand new town, filled with same old faces
Tires getting thin, destination unknown places

Never knew how old I'd feel, after so few years on earth
Thinking of a better day, and dreaming of re-birth
But a stirring in my head, filled with sounds I can't control
Train whistle blowing hard, calling me to come back home

She stopped and I was stuck on what to do next. When she started into a quiet cry, I stepped back. Right or wrong, I left her alone. From the little I knew about her, it was a place she was used to.

***

The race started later and I blotted out the images Renee left behind. I didn't know what to make of the song but when I started a steady stride my breathing took over. I stayed in a pack of runners and was content to hide out right in the middle. Even though I wasn't very tired, it was a nice, safe place to be. When I neared the tennis courts I looked toward the clump of trees where Renee had been. She was long gone but her voice still echoed in my head. For a second I was distracted and nearly fell over a root jutting from the ground. It was only when two Billys yelled from the practice football field that I regained my focus.

"Don't fall on your face, loser," one called.

"Nice shorts, you bunch of fags," shouted another.

Their voices were like electrical wires to my gonads and the jolt of adrenaline lit my system.

Assholes! I wanted to call back but saved my breath and pushed harder. The harder I ran, the angrier I got. I ran like a crazed lunatic as if the hot beads of sweat were spikes of glass spurring me on. I purposely jammed the pain into the black hole I had visited so many times before. Out of the corner of my eye, I saw my coach waving his arms and yelling like a crazy-man on crystal meth. All I could hear was the blood swooshing through my head as I pounded over the course. I ran full-tilt until I neared the final flags marking the finish line. My breath came in raw gasps and sounded like a wounded animal just waiting to be put out of his misery. When I crossed the finish line, in some ways that's exactly what I was.

"You were second?" said Curt with bugged eyes when he finished a minute later. "What the hell was that?"

With my hands still on my knees, I spat a load of white, foamy phlegm toward the ground. I waited a few seconds until my breathing edged backed toward a manageable range. "What do you mean?" I asked in a hoarse voice.

"I mean it looked like you were going to kill somebody out there."

"Only if they got in my way," I said in my best attempt to sound like a natural born killer. I walked over to the side and reset placed my hands on my slick knees feeling a little proud of myself.

"A true beast," said a new voice. "Quite impressive. I never knew you had it in you," she said as a hand was placed on my back.

I didn't even look up and knew it was Renee. She had watched from somewhere in the distance.

"You spying on me like all the other hot babes?" I asked as the sweat dripped in my eyes. I straightened up and tried to focus through the stinging salt.

She shook her head happily. "You should be proud of yourself. You did great."

I squinted at her and my tongue got stuck in my throat.

She shrugged and jumped back in. "I was around and saw a bunch of skinny guys running. So I just watched." She paused and a smile covered her face. "You're really fast," she said.

I was embarrassed and the splotchy color on my cheeks turned a shade darker. "Something just got into me," I said as I chose not to explain any further.

"Something indeed," she replied.

***

I invited Curt and Renee over to my house that night so we could just hang out. I even promised we could use the hot tub if they wanted to soak. My mom and dad would be gone and to be honest, I just felt like doing *something*. When the doorbell rang hours later, I froze up like a pound of beef at the Piggly Wiggly. I wasn't used to having friends over and I breathed slowly to steady my nerves. I heard them talking and through the window caught a glimpse of Curt's old rusted Honda. He inherited the car from his old hippie uncle who kept the thing together with bailing wire and duct tape.

"Coming," I said as I battled with the dead bolt.

"Hey, pretty-boy," said Renee as the door swung open. "What's up?"

I smiled back and nodded to Curt as he stood behind her.

"Uhh," I said with a shrug. "Just chillin' for awhile." I tried to play it cool but felt as see-through as a plate glass window. I backed up a step and waved them in.

Renee stopped short and let out a low whistle. "Holy freakin' crap!" she said. "Nice place, Ritchie Rich. Do you mind if a few peasants come in?"

I followed her eyes toward the original paintings and the freshly polished cherry furniture decorating the front room. I withheld the uncomfortable fact that Rosa the fat cleaning lady had left only hours earlier.

"Just don't sneeze," I said closing the door behind them. "My mom will call a fumigator to kill the germs. I feel like I live in a hospital."

Renee nodded. "I'll hold my breath. I wouldn't want to infect the intensive care ward." She set a small nylon bag on the floor and spread her arms wide. "So we got the place to ourselves? Nobody home?"

"No." I said hesitantly. "Both of my parents are working late. It's just me and the fish."

She nodded and let the air out of her lungs as if she was letting out pressure. "Can we get a grand tour?"

I wasn't prepared for the request. I thought they would come over and we'd hop into the Jacuzzi and just hang out. I had no real reason to say no so I mumbled out a response. "Sure, I suppose." Curt had been over a few times before so the show was for Renee only. "I guess we can go upstairs and see my room."

"As good a place as any to start," she said.

"He's got a kick-ass computer in his room. Awesome graphics," added Curt.

"It's okay," I stammered. "Good for gaming, I guess." I lead them up the steps but Renee stopped halfway and admired the pictures on the wall.

"Is this you?" she asked. "You were so cute!"

Because I was an only child I had no way out so I came clean. "Yeah, that's me. I fought like hell when they made me wear that purple polka dot bow tie and the short pants. I really pitched a shit. Literally."

"I'm sure," said Curt. "You were a happenin' dude back then. Whatever happened?"

"Testosterone. Ever hear of it?"

Renee smiled. "I think you looked great. You're mom has good taste in clothes. You look like a prince in the making."

"That's debatable," I said. "But if I ever have a kid I promise I won't make him wear clothes that make him look like the son of a flaming English sailor. He'll be all man, I promise you that. All beef diet, all the time."

She nodded and we continued up the steps. "I'm sure he'll be quite the stud just like his daddy."

"Undoubtedly," I promised and lead them down the long hallway toward my bedroom. That was before Renee stopped and took a look inside my parent's room.

"Wow," she said under her breath. "This is amazing."

I honestly never even thought about it. When your home is all you've ever known you don't question how it got there. It just is. Just as much as the blue sky overhead or the wind in your face. Now that she pointed it out, I realized she was right. The antique four-post king-sized bed stood front and center in the room. Maybe I was weird but it gave me a sudden image of a princess removing her chastity belt just before being railed on by some horny king. The oversized fan spun from the ceiling and the picture window let the dying light of the day stream into the room. The light twinkled on the blue-green walls that my parents had debated about for weeks on end. Agua, I think my mom called the color when they made the final epic decision that was sure to rock the western world.

"It's weird looking at my parent's bedroom," I told her as I moved towards my own. "I can't think about … stuff."

"Understood," said Curt.

Even Renee nodded, but it didn't stop her from taking one last look around. I led them into my room and waved my right hand into the air. The room wasn't in the best of shape, but at least I had picked up the boxer shorts that usually lay piled up in the corners. The bed was unmade and the other main piece of equipment was the computer hutch where I spent most of my time. I had recently gotten a bigger flat screen monitor and the box it came in stood next to the desk.

"Nice," said Renee. "I've never had a computer of my own."

Curt looked at me and we each waited for the other one to answer. When he shrugged it was left up to me.

"Never?" I asked. I was surprised because I could never remember *not* having a computer. Not for one minute of my conscious memory. I instantly felt bad when I remembered bitching about my last monitor until I was able to guilt my parents into buying me the latest and greatest.

"No," she continued. "I usually use the ones at the library. Once my mom got an old one from a friend, but we never had Internet. I played the games that were installed, but that was about it."

"At least it was something," offered Curt.

It was nice he tried to make Renee feel better but for whatever reason I felt worse. She soaked in the rest of my room and I decided it was time to move on.

"Anyone still feel like the hot tub?" I asked.

Curt helped me out when he nodded.

"I know I am. Been looking forward to it all night."

Renee looked around the room one last time as if memorizing the layout. Then she answered slowly. "Right."

I guessed she would have spent the night in my bedroom just enjoying the view.

***

We made our way down the steps and headed toward the patio door. I followed Renee as she looked around and for a moment I questioned inviting her over. I was uncomfortable knowing I had so much more than she did and deep down realized I didn't appreciate it as much as I should. But she was here and it was too late now. I did my best to pretend I was up for whatever lay ahead and I motioned toward the deck.

"The Jacuzzi is right out back. You guys sure?"

Curt nodded enthusiastically like a bobble-head doll. "Dang right. I haven't been in one of those since I was ten. My Aunt Marilyn got married and we stayed in a Holiday Inn. I got sick that night. Too many kiddie cocktails."

"A real party animal," I said.

"A wild man," seconded Renee. Then she looked out the window towards the backyard. "I've never even been in a Jacuzzi. I've only seen them on TV."

I attempted to pump up the conversation. "I've been trying to get on *Real Life*."

"Oh, yeah?" asked Curt knowing I was full of shit. "Tell me about it."

"Well, my biggest problem is I'm not sure of what my role should be. The rich kid, the bitch, the gay dude, the punk or the drunk," I said. "Or should I have sex or not."

"I didn't think that was your choice," said Curt. "Or you would be doing it like a dog."

He was right but I didn't admit it. Lucky Renee jumped in.

"It's like showing the world how screwed up you are. No thanks," said Renee. "I'll keep that to myself."

I laughed but didn't know if I should have. Serious conversation hadn't crossed my path much over the years so I didn't always react quickly.

"You seem like you're doing okay to me," I said. Her look said otherwise, but nothing was said until I spoke again. "Let's hit the tub," I said. "My parents could be home anytime. God help us."

***

Renee changed into what passed for a swimsuit. It was more a pair of shorts and a sports bra that had seen better days. It made me realize how she normally dressed—jeans and a white t-shirt. Nothing more. At first I thought it was a punky fashion statement until I realized it might be about all she had. Somehow, it made me like her all the more. She set a coke down on the edge of the tub and slipped into the water. Given the situation, I did my best not to get a good look. When she glared at me, it was immediately obvious I had failed miserably.

70

"You can stop checking me out anytime now," she ordered as she settled in. "God, I hate that."

"I … I … uhh …" I stuttered.

"You were. You know it. And it's annoying."

I looked at Curt for help, but he was oblivious as usual and I was left on my own. He seemed to be enjoying the jets hitting his back and I suspected he was trying to squeeze out a few well-placed farts. So I thought of how to get her to understand, but knew she never would. No woman possibly could. Regardless, I decided to come clean.

"Maybe I can explain," I said.

"Please do," she replied.

"You want me to be honest?"

"As Abe Lincoln," she urged.

I swallowed hard. "Well, I can't speak for Abe, but I think boobs look like a lot of fun. Like something that should be … should be …"

"Spit it out, perv," she urged.

"Should be played with," I blurted.

She stared at me with a look that blended pity with amazement. That was soon replaced by one of disdain shrink-wrapped in disgust.

"Played with?" she repeated. "I think maybe I heard you wrong."

"You asked," I said honestly. As the bubbles settled over my chest, I plowed ahead. "I mean if I was a girl, I swear I would never get anything done. I'd probably play with myself all day. It would be awesome."

Her face crinkled and tiny lines appeared at the corner of her dark eyes. "That just might be the stupidest thing anyone's ever said. Actually, it is the stupidest thing anyone has ever *thought*! I take back what I said about you the first day we met."

"What was that?"

"That you were smart. I must have been mistaken."

"It could be that I'm both smart *and* horny. Did you ever think of that?"

She shook her head and a few drops of water fell from her wet hair. "No I didn't," she admitted. "I don't get boys. Maybe I never will. They think more with their nuts than their brains. Maybe the two are linked by some weird nerve."

"I have no answer to that," I said and looked to Curt for help. "Help me out here," I urged. When he grunted out a non-response, I suspected he was too busy releasing a few more bubbles into the water.

"Say what?" he asked as he lifted his head up. "I was relaxing."

"If you relax any harder, we'll probably have to clear out," I said. Renee looked at me and I gambled that a quick change of topic was in order. "So what do you think of Greendale so far? And ignore any pervs that you might have just recently met."

She slid down further. "No better, no worse than other places," she said over the bubbling water. "People are the same everywhere."

"Meaning?"

"Meaning everybody *thinks* they got it all going on, but they're really all the same. Just the faces and addresses change."

"Not that different from Nebraska?"

"Or San Diego. Or Salt Lake City, Houston or Saint Louis just to name a few."

"I take it you've lived in all those places," I said. "So why did you move so much? Your dad's job?"

"My mom's," she said with a shrug. "Among other things."

"What does your mom do?" asked Curt as he unexpectedly entered into the conversation.

She swallowed hard. "She was a dancer. And not a showgirl in Las Vegas if you know what I mean." She took a long drink of her coke and set it back on the edge. "But dancing and men go together." She looked up at the starlit sky and shrugged. "She sacked up with more than a few. Probably hoping they would love her and take her away to a better place. In the end one of her Prince Charmings left her three steps behind with a kid. And somewhere out west is some guy with half my DNA. Probably spreading more whenever he gets a chance."

I stared straight ahead and hoped Curt wouldn't say anything. To my surprise, he nodded knowingly without saying anything stupid. So I tried my best to steer the ship.

"Sorry, Renee," I said in a weak voice. "I don't know what to say to that." I thought for a second. "Did you ever meet your dad?"

She shook her head. "No. The fact is I'm not even sure my mom knows exactly who he is. How sad is that?"

I definitely had no answer.

"It's not the best," I said in a massive understatement. "So it's just been you and her I guess."

"Pretty much so. Except for the three or four times she thought she was in love."

"It never worked out?" The answer was obvious but the words hung in the air as thick as steam from the tub.

"No. But it was worse when she was living with them. When they broke up we got kicked out and would move to another town where my mom could find work. Until the next time."

"That really sucks, Renee," said Curt. "I can't even imagine. I get mad at my dad when he's late to pick me up after student council. Now that makes me feel pretty stupid."

I agreed with Curt but didn't say anything. Renee shrugged helplessly and lost herself in the bubbles.

"Why did your mom leave?" I asked. "I mean, why are you with your aunt?"

"Do you have to know everything?" she said in a voice that suddenly turned angry. "You a cop?"

Curt and I looked at each other. Then Renee spoke again before I could get a word out.

"Sorry. That wasn't fair."

I sort of shrugged her anger away. "I was just asking," I explained. "I didn't mean to pry. It's your life and all."

"My life," she repeated. "I guess you could call it that." Her black hair soaked up the warm water and floated on the surface like a drowned rat. She closed her eyes before opening them again. "My mom is complicated. She tries to do the right thing most of the time, but whenever she stands up she gets knocked down again. Or knocked up." She laughed at her own joke. Then she was quiet as the Jacuzzi hummed in the background. "She made me promise I would get a good education. So when she talked to my aunt she begged her to take me in because the schools are good here. At the very least there would be a roof over my head."

"She just left you here?" Curt asked incredulously.

"No. She stayed a few weeks until I got settled in. When she left she promised she would be back soon. But I'm not holding my breath." She looked up into the black of the night. "I think she just needed to breathe on her own and not be smothered by a weight of fifteen years."

"You're not a weight," I insisted. "That's not being fair to yourself."

"Maybe," she replied. "But it's hard not to think that way. Really hard."

I hadn't expected things to get so heavy and I blew out some air. The steam from the hot tub blended in until it disappeared from view. I did my best to salvage the night and tried to spin a positive.

"You're here now, right? A fresh start," I said. "Maybe that's what you need more than anything."

She shrugged and stared at the water. Then she turned and smiled at me with moist eyes that said everything and nothing at the same time. "Maybe. But it sure leaves me feeling like I'm riding life solo. Sometimes I think that's a good thing." She poked at a foamy bubble that reached the surface. "Sometimes not."

I had no immediate response. I was quiet and looked around and felt guilty over everything I had. Including parents.

"So now you are living with your aunt," I stated. "What is she like?"

She shrugged. "Tired. Depressed. With a husband and a kid. I share a room with a six-year-old boy. He's cool, but it's still pretty weird. I suppose it's better than sleeping in the back of a car."

Curt then decided to get into the act. "So where is your mom now?"

"It doesn't really matter," she said. "I guess she's somewhere near Seattle. Or maybe San Francisco." She took another drink of her coke. "I'm better off without her. Maybe I'll get to stay here until I graduate."

I could almost feel the wishful thinking float in the air just as much as the steam surrounding us. As long as she was game, I kept on. "Do you have any contact with her? Does she call at all?"

"Not too often," she said firmly. "As each day goes by I think of her as less my mother and more like somebody who spit me out when I was ripe." She splashed at the water. "The funny thing is she's with me every day. I inherited a few things from her."

"Inherited?" asked Curt. "That sounds like a good thing."

She smiled the saddest smile I had ever seen and her eyes flickered like the last embers of a dying fire. Then she spoke slowly. "Sometimes you inherit both good and bad. Most times you wish for neither."

"What does that mean?" I asked.

She looked at me before raising her eyes to the skies.

"Some other time," she said. "I just don't want to think anymore."

I swallowed and before I could even reply, my mom's voice exploded from behind.

"Well, I'll be a monkey's uncle. And its grandmother too," she said. "Just what do we have here?"

I closed my eyes as if I could squeeze away the moment. *Dammit!* I thought. But my words came out a bit different.

"Mom," I said in a flat voice. "You're home early."

"Slow day at the office. Better luck tomorrow," she said as if it was a personal prayer. She looked over the hot tub before a curious look crossed her face. "So who are your friends?"

"I think you know Curt," I said. "And this is Renee."

"Hi, Curt," she said, "I know we've met before." She lowered her eyes and I waited. "Hello, Renee. You must be a new friend of Jimmy's. I've never heard him speak of a pretty girl before." She extended her hand as if she was making a business deal.

Renee took it and looked into my mom's eyes. Then she smiled slowly. "Yes," she answered with what I thought was a slight blush. "I just moved here."

"Oh. Where do you live?"

"Near the high school," I chimed in. I knew what my mom was thinking, but it was too late.

"In one of those cute Greendale Originals? Those hold their value so well."

"No," said Renee. "In the apartments."

"I see," said my mom as she stood up and let go of Renee's hand. She brightened up when Renee kept on.

"The problem is it's too crowded for my two brothers and the dogs. We need more space. We're looking to buy a four-bedroom home with a fireplace. Maybe even a pool," she added as an afterthought.

I was both embarrassed and confused. She had created a family out of thin air and at first I thought she was jacking my mom around, but then I saw the faraway look in her eyes and knew better. Maybe it was her dream. A dream that was probably as loose as a feather in the wind.

"How funny," said my mom as dollar bills damn near floated down from above. "I just listed a place like that today," she said. "Near a park, which would be perfect for the dogs. It has an in-ground pool that would certainly help the house retain its value. I would be happy to show it to your parents sometime."

Renee suddenly looked as if she had a film over her eyes just like my grandpa before he had cataract surgery. She gazed into the sky and a longing covered her face like a thin veil.

"I'll tell my mom and dad. I'm sure they'll be in touch."

76

My mom beamed and took a step back.

"I'll leave you kids alone," she said. "Let me know if you need anything."

She left to go inside and I was more confused than ever. When Renee's looked at me I got the heebie-jeebies on the back of my neck. Then she closed her eyes and slipped under the water and it seemed like the hum of the Jacuzzi doubled. For that moment, I let everything pass like the bubbles that churned in the night.

Chapter Six
In My Head

The week started like any other. Crawling out of bed Monday morning and hating every step toward the bathroom. Bad hair and a face that looked like it had been used for a dartboard. I would go to bed with a semi-clean face and wake up to skin that looked like Mount Vesuvius springing a leak. It wasn't a picnic knowing that at any time a new zit could appear and say hello to the world. The problem was the general population usually got to see it before I did.

"Incoming," I said to the splattered mirror that recorded the ungodly truth.

The only good part of the week was the daily lunch. As sad a commentary as that was it was my reality. The Hot Table had no interest in us for the moment and I was happy for the peace. The aura of their greatness was always lurking in the scent of pizza and french fries dominating the air, but I guessed the Killer B's had lesser bugs to step on at the moment.

"Where's Curt?" Renee asked as she sat down.

"Some egg-head club meeting," I said. "Only the hard boiled were invited."

"That leaves me out," she said.

"Me too. Most times I don't even want to be part of stuff like that but other times …" I said as I opened my lunch and didn't finish the sentence.

"What?" she asked.

"It's nothing," I told her. "Just stupid stuff."

"If it's stupid then tell me," she insisted.

"Well," I started, "I was just in the bathroom and I heard some guys talking. A bunch of Billys."

"And?" she said in a voice that sounded like my mothers.

I decided it didn't matter so I plowed ahead. "I already told you about the Billys and the Beez. But I never told you about a secret one I just heard about. It's kind of gross."

"Now you got me, bro. Spill it."

"There's a shit one on campus here," I said as I looked around as if I was being bugged. "It's called the Gritch Club." I had her attention so I kept on. "The guys get points for how far they get with girls. So they try to get with as many girls as they can. They add up the points each quarter and throw a party for the winner. The leading scorer you might say."

"That's disgusting," Renee said.

"I know. I heard a rumor about it last year but now I'm sure."

"Why is that?"

I did my best to explain. "I was doing my deal in the bathroom and I know no one thought I was there. A bunch of Billys were bragging about the weekend. Adding up their points."

"You've got to be kidding," she said.

"I wish I was but I'm not."

"Go on."

"Well, they have a Facebook page that they keep up with pictures and everything. They even give bonus points for certain girls. The ones that they call the 'Ice Queens'. I can't get on the page but I guess there's a lot of nasty shit on it. At least that's what they said."

She looked at me before she glared at The Hot Table. She was so heated a smoke detector would have gone off if it had been over her head.

"We have to do something about that," she said and placed a hand on my shoulder.

"We?"

"Yes. That's so gross it makes me angry. It's like they think girls are like cattle." She stopped talking as her head dipped and her hair dropped over her eyes. She looked more pissed than I had ever seen her. Then she straightened up and laser beamed me one more time. "You need to get inside and take those guys down. For real."

I stiffened and my lips locked up again.

"But, but—"

"But what?"

What did she want me to be? I thought. *Some kind of freakin' James Bond with my Dr. Pepper shaken, not stirred?*

"That's crazy. I'm just, just—"

"Afraid? Screw the James Bond shit. Just be a man!" she said.

I jumped from my chair and nearly fell on my face. "No freakin' way. Not again!"

"What?" she said.

I could tell she knew exactly what I meant.

"You know! Like you're inside my head! It's … it's … too freakin' weird." I tried to chill but it was no use. I was losing it and she knew it.

"Sit down, Jimmy," she said quietly as she looked around. I didn't move so she said it again. "Please. I mean it." Then she said one last thing. "I'll try to explain."

That got my attention so I sat down. Before I did I pulled the chair to a safe distance.

"Go ahead."

She lowered her voice. "I don't know how to start."

It wasn't like she was at a loss of words ever before.

"Just tell me," I said. I wanted to know at the same time that I didn't.

"I have this thing."

"Thing?"

"Yes. Thing." She looked around again. "But you'll think I'm crazy," she said and turned away.

"Tell me," I said louder.

She breathed deep and plunged ahead. "I can tell what somebody is thinking if I touch them." She shrugged as if she was helpless. "Or if they touch me. It's been that way since I was little." She looked at me as if she was waiting for me to laugh or make fun of her. When I just stared she kept on. "It just happens and I can't explain it."

I grunted out an earth-shattering reply. "Ummm," I said.

She nodded. "Yeah. That's what I thought you would say. But worse is what you're thinking."

I swallowed and tried to say something. Anything. Then I mumbled out all I could. "That's too ... that's too weird to believe." Then I thought of the few times she had pulled the words out of my head. I remembered each time she had been close to me. Touching me. "When you touch?" I said as I leaned away from her. Now it made sense at the same time that it didn't. I looked straight at her and considered that she was shitting me. Then she reached out and touched my forearm as I stiffened in my chair. Her eyes lit up until she let go.

"No Jimmy. I wouldn't shit you," she said.

Before I knew it I flipped back in my chair and fell on my ass. I saw stars but realized they were just the lights overhead.

"Jimmy! Are you okay?" she said as she jumped from her chair and knelt beside me.

I was fine except for being embarrassed. I straightened up the chair and pretended that it was defective but realized hardly anyone had even noticed. I slithered back on the chair and acted as cool as I could considering the circumstances.

"I ... I," I said.

"I never should have told you," she interrupted. "I knew you would never understand."

I suddenly wished I was at Curt's brainiac meeting instead of with Renee but that didn't matter now. So I did the best I could.

"I do and I don't," I said. I regrouped until my breathing return to normal. When I got my feet under me I couldn't resist being a smart ass again. "So tell me more. Does it work all the time? Do I turn into a zombie after you're done? Or maybe I turn into a freaking werewolf?"

"I'm not from another planet," she said in a high voice that was close to being pissed off. "It … it just happens."

"Let's try it," I challenged her.

"Right here? Right now?" she said as she looked around the cafeteria.

"Why not? Chickenshit?"

"No. Never," she said.

"Then pull a Nike and just do it."

She didn't disagree and she moved her elbow to touch my forearm. "Fine. If you're going to be that way about it. Just this once."

I was surprised she agreed and I readied myself. "Okay," I said, "what am I thinking now?"

Renee looked at me just before she scrunched up her nose. "Jimmy, really. That lunch lady? You've got to be kidding."

"Just wait!" I said before she almost pulled away. "Try again."

She looked into my eyes and I my head did a slow rumble. "That's even worse, Jimmy. You got the hots for that bitch Veronica too? Get in line with the other losers."

"Never mind," I said as I tried to control my voice. I had to admit I was shaking inside but I had one final test for her before I finished. "Last time."

She looked at me and I tried to ignore her eyes but they drew me in. Then she yanked her arm back like she had been shocked by a wire. "My eyes aren't black," she said. "They're really dark brown." She looked away from me like she was embarrassed. "I don't want to do this anymore."

She had hit three for three and the hair on the back of my neck stood up. "Okay," I said. "That's enough. You were right on." I had no clue what to say next. "So you're like a superhero. What am I supposed to say to that?"

82

"Don't be a dick, Jimmy," she blurted. "I didn't choose this. You think I like having some random guy at the store bump up against me and I know he's cheating on his wife? Or that some kid hates his dad because he beat the shit out of him a few hours ago?" She breathed deep and shook her head. "It's not a talent, Jimmy. It's a fucking curse and it's kept me from ever feeling a part of anything. I purposely stay away from people because of what I might find out." Her eyes got misty. "Do you know how many times I lay next to my mom when I was little and could feel her desperation? How I knew we were broke and that we had no money for the bills? I was just a kid!" She wiped at her eyes. "I wish I never had it."

It was then I knew it was a piece of herself she needed to keep hidden forever. We all had secrets that grew in the dark corners of our minds like toadstools in a forbidden forest but hers were way bigger than mine might ever be.

"Did I ever tell you I played trombone in the fifth grade?" I asked her.

"What? What does that have to do with anything?"

"I know it's a random thought. Actually completely random. There is a point though."

"Okay," she said. "I hope it'll be worth it."

I looked at The Hot Table and tried to explain. "I flunked out of band when the teacher discovered I faked playing and never even blew a note during the concerts. My arms were too short and my lips too thin. I couldn't even make it in band! How sad it that?"

"Very. But I still don't see the point."

"The point is I have never been much a part of anything. Sort of like you. I'm alone too," I said. "We're the same. Except that I can't get into heads like you can."

"Don't remind me."

"So we're not so different if you really think about it. I mean I've been on my own for as long as I can remember. I haven't felt connected anywhere for just about forever."

"So what do we do now?" she asked, "now that you know?"

I didn't have an answer and didn't pretend that I did. I chewed on my sandwich as I tried to find the words that never came. She looked at me and it was all I could do to swallow.

We sat in silence until the bell rang. When we walked together to Mrs. Spoon's class Renee finally broke the ice.

"I'll see you after school. Please?"

She looked like she was about to cry so I did the only thing I could.

I nodded my head.

***

We met by the tennis courts and sat against the metal fence. I felt like it was my turn to start. So I did my best.

"So … so, I think we were talking about … well, you know what I'm going to say."

I guessed that pissed her off a little. "It's not that way at all, Jimmy. Saying a thing like that is why I've never told anyone besides my mom."

"What did she say?"

"She didn't believe me." She shrugged. "Why should she? Who would want a freak for a daughter?"

I shook my head. "You're not a freak. Just … just really, really different. If you really think about it, it's kind of awesome. Sort of sets you apart from the crowd, wouldn't you say?"

She gave a little laugh and things lightened up.

"Slightly. Like by about a mile."

"When did you first know?"

"At first I thought it was the same for everyone. That somehow people just knew things about other people. Then way back," she began to explain. "I remember holding my teacher's hand and a thought of hers jumped into my head. So I asked her about it."

"What was it?"

"She was looking at the gym teacher and I asked her what a 'tight ass' was. I remember her almost falling over. She called my mom and told her. After that I got a little more careful about what I knew."

"Do you use it a lot? I mean do you use it on purpose?"

She looked away but answered quickly. "I use it sometimes but deep down I know it's not right, you know? So I try not to. Most times it just happens when it happens and I don't even think about it much." Then she turned to face me. "You can't tell anyone. No one at all."

I almost choked on my tongue. "Why tell me?" I croaked.

She didn't hesitate. "Because I haven't had a real friend in a long time."

I was shocked and happy at the same time. I had my own short list of friends so I knew what she was feeling.

"I'm honored, I guess." Then I ran out of words. "So now what?"

"There's no 'now what'. We'll just see what happens." She looked at me. "You have to promise that you won't tell anyone. Not even Curt."

Shit! I thought. *No one?* I hadn't planned on telling the school newspaper, but I was almost drooling waiting to let this one rip. Then a second later I knew she was right. If it got out in the school she'd be torn apart from seventeen directions. So I gave her my word.

"I promise. If you promise not to tell anyone I once had a wet dream about a nun. Sister Agnes, I think."

"Really?"

"No," I told her. "I just thought it would just give you something to hold over me just in case."

"You're weird. But I'm glad."

So it was settled. She was a superpowered babe and I was her trusted sidekick. I was going to suggest we give ourselves nicknames when the football team came out and ran toward the field. Leading the way was the usual suspects of Rex and Vance.

"There go the boys. U-rah-rah and all that shit," I said.

"Screw that. Maybe we should really shake up the school," she said. "Like from inside out."

"How? Turn terrorist? Pull a Columbine?"

She shook her head and watched the players run by. "No not at all. But maybe we get inside. Like you get to be a Billy."

"That'll happen," I said. "Like I'm Billy material."

"Maybe you just need to man up, Jimmy."

That hurt. Really hurt.

"Man up to what? To be a Billy? That's a shitty thing to say."

"That's not the way I meant it. What I mean is get in the Gritch Club in order to blow it up. All the way. Expose them for the pricks that they are."

"So I stick my neck out? For what?"

"To do the right thing. To let this town know that everything isn't the way it seems. That all of the heroes and princesses are full of shit and in the end no one is any better than anyone else. That we have just as much right as anyone else in this town to belong, Jimmy. You and me both."

I nodded and shook my head. A hum overtook my brain and I wasn't sure if I was short-circuiting there on the spot. So I waited a few seconds. "So I just embarrass myself and try to get in the club? Maybe get my ass kicked? What about you? What will you do?"

"I'll do what I can do. Or you can use me as an in. Like an admission ticket to the party."

I had no idea what that meant.

"What?"

"Vance was hot on me, right? And Rex would hump a dead log if he could get off. Tell them what you want about me and we'll get you in. I guarantee it."

"That's dangerous. Way too much."

"Life is dangerous. Maybe those assholes will get what's coming to them. Even better, we do it together. I promise."

86

She was asking a lot more than I could give at the moment but I was too numbed to say much more.

"I'll think about it," I lied. In fact, I wanted nothing to do with it.

"Don't let life pass you by," she warned. "What do you have to lose anyway?"

"About two pints of blood and a row of teeth," I said. I stood up and started walking away. I'm already late for cross country," I said. "I got to run."

"Then run, Jimmy. Run."

I didn't turn back as my neck muscles turned to steel.

***

The weekend hit and I couldn't get Renee's words out of my head. The fact that she could literally *get* in my head and now she wanted more of me than I was prepared to offer. Me in the Gritch Club? *Not a chance,* said my deepest and darkest brainwaves. The worst thing was the thought just wouldn't go away. I couldn't even concentrate on my gaming and that's when I knew it was really, really bad. Lately my cyberfriends seemed almost more real to me than my classmates. In fact some guy in my guild wanted me to come to West Virginia and hang out. I think he's just a kid like me, but in a world full of sick twists you never know. I'd probably get there and he'd be some hairy 40 year-old, three hundred pound walrus-dude that would like to cuddle me like a juicy teddy bear. It sucks to think about that stuff, but weirder shit happens every day.

So the hours went by and I wasted time on the computer. Then I did something I never thought I would do. I went online and searched the Gritch Club. It was protected but I took a step as big as the Grand Canyon and asked to be friended. I'm not sure why but I did and a second later I regretted it. The shitty thing about computers is you can't take it back once you've hit the magic key.

So I stared at the screen and felt so far over my head I was leaving blue sky and entering into the black. I felt about as stupid as the time I thought my fifth grade teacher was hot for me. Turns out she was a lezbo. Who would have guessed?

***

Monday morning always sucked the worst because there was nothing to look forward to and the weekend seemed, well, five days away. I pushed through the front doors and entered what I called "Shadowland" - a place set squarely between the cool kids and the social rejects on life support systems. I lived there for a year now and each day I hoped to make it through without being crushed like a potato chip on the lunchroom floor. I had always hung on by my fingernails but since I met Renee I was like some African native dancing on hot coals. Now on my own I had stuck my skinny neck into the business of the Billys and their hormone-fueled scoring machine.

I almost tiptoed down the hallway and tried to hide from the Killer B's. That changed the second I passed by the sophomore pole and a giant frizz appeared. His hair was crazier than usual but I'm sure he didn't give a shit. Actually he probably liked it that way. I had never realized it but he had a little birthmark on his neck that resembled a tiny flower. Imagine that, a sensitive spot engrained on Rex direct from God's hand. That image didn't last long when he spoke.

"So *you* want in, little man" he said in a voice too loud. "For real?"

I froze. I almost stuttered, but I choked back the words jammed in my throat. Instead I nodded and waited to get laughed at, but a strange thing happened. Four more Billys stepped forward and surrounded me.

"You got balls to ask in. Big-time balls," said Vance with a sneer that nearly echoed in the air. Heads bobbed in agreement and I bit my tongue so it wouldn't drop from my mouth. "What do you got to offer?'"

I had no answer immediately and I swallowed. "I umm—"

Rex jumped in again. "A lot of guys want in. We need something to see if you're worthy."

A few Billys nodded in agreement until Vance came closer.

"He's friends with that new girl. The one that gets in Veronica's face all the time," he said. "She's worth something. Maybe extra points."

"I ... I ... I," I started to say before I stopped my stuttering by biting down hard on my tongue. "I know her," I said nonchalantly.

"Is she *available*?" Rex asked in a way that made me way past uncomfortable.

"She's not ... not my girlfriend," I sputtered. "We just met." Suddenly I felt like a Judas giving up the goods.

"Fair game then?" Rex said aloud. "You got anything else? A good car, maybe?"

I swallowed my hairball and for the first time noticed a faded barbwire tattoo that looked like it had been done by some random Billy with a nail and an ink pen. But I sure as hell didn't say that when I spoke. "Not exactly," I said. "My dad owns the used car lot on Loomis Road. He would give you a deal if you say you know me." Actually, I wasn't sure that was the case and I felt dirtier the moment the words left my mouth.

"I like that. I need new wheels," said Rex as he moved in so close I could smell his musk-scented body wash. "Maybe we'll give you a go." Vance shrugged and Rex whispered in a deep voice. "There's a party at the lake this weekend. You're invited if you bring your friend. Think of it as a test run."

The bell rang and broke the spell. I stood still as if I had been turned to stone.

***

I didn't say a word to anyone about the invitation all week. Maybe I hoped I would somehow forget about the party and then wouldn't have to deal with it. Of course that was about as likely to happen as me growing a pecker on my forehead. None of that mattered when Renee sat down at lunch Friday and blurted out the secret I had tried to keep bound and gagged.

"Are you going to the party tonight?" she asked as we sat down in the cafeteria. "I heard about it a little while ago."

"What?" I asked as I spit up a hunk of half-chewed bologna. "Who told you about it?"

"So you knew about it too?" she asked.

"I heard a rumor," I lied. "Where did you hear that from?"

"Some guy invited me. I'm not even sure of his name. He had on a football jersey though."

"A Billy, I'd guess."

"Could be. Who told you?" she asked.

I hesitated. Then I spit it out cold turkey. "I'm trying to get in the Gritch Club. Online. Just like you talked about."

"You what?" said Curt. "You've got to be kidding."

My face boiled over. "I did it just to get on the inside. Renee and I had an idea to bust it up. But first I need to get in."

"Who are you all of a sudden? Secret Agent Boy?" Curt asked. "That's about the stupidest idea ever."

I looked at Renee for help and she jumped right in.

"Maybe, Curt. But you got to stand up sometime. Right and wrong and all that bullshit."

"Yeah," I said weakly. I waited but no one said anything so I continued. "Rex told me about the party," I paused again. "It's like my audition for the club, I guess."

"What do you have to do?" asked Curt clearly annoyed. "Smooth some girl and bring back her thong as an offering to the gods?"

"Don't be an ass, Curt."

"Everyone knows what they do," he replied. "Worse is that some girls don't even seem to care."

"Yeah, well. When I don't get in then it's over." I took a small bite of my sandwich. "We'll just see what happens."

"Exactly," said Renee. "Maybe we'll all be surprised. Either way it's better than just sitting around doing nothing." She bit around a bruise on her apple and spoke again. "So what time is the party?"

I was a million miles away and grunted out a non-reply. Renee took it as confusion to the question.

"The party," she repeated. "At the lake."

I re-focused. "Whenever it gets dark. They only come out at night," I said. "Maybe Curt can drive."

I looked at Curt while he wiped a dot of Coke off the caterpillar sitting on his upper lip. When he realized I was waiting he sputtered out a reply.

"Drive to a party? Me?" He paused and re-armed himself. "You been smokin' something?"

I had never been to a high school party and expected this year would be the same. In fact, the last party I had been to was in seventh grade where we watched movies and ate junk food all night. I remember waking up next to a little orange barf-pile of Cheetos courtesy of some fat kid who plowed through a whole bag of nacho style. To this day I can't walk down the snack aisle in the grocery store without gacking a little bit.

"No he hasn't, Curt," said Renee jolting me back to the present. "It might even be fun."

I disagreed. Sort of. "My grandpa used to say, 'If you put barbecue sauce on a shit sandwich, it still tastes like shit'."

"What's that supposed to mean?" asked Curt.

I shook my head and spelled it out for him. "It means that Renee is making the party seem better than it is."

She lasered me and my balls scrunched up. "You are in high school, aren't you?" she asked.

"Well, yeah."

"Then it's for you, isn't it?" she said straight out.

"Well, there are high schoolers and then there are *high schoolers*," I attempted to explain. Renee knew exactly what I meant.

"Screw them," she said as piss dripped off her voice. "It might be interesting. Like observing a different species. One that someday we'll all be a part of."

My heart beat faster. Actually raced is more like it. I'm not sure she had any idea what a steaming pile she was leading us into. I imagined it squishing under our feet and smelling like a septic tank but I was too chickenshit to say anything more about it.

"You're not afraid, are you?" she said as she smelled my fear. Then she moved closer.

"Don't you touch me," I warned.

She stopped as if she had gotten stung. I ignored her for a second and listened to the hum of the cafeteria. Like a crazed swarm of Brazilian bees just waiting to attack the next nectar-covered victim and felt as if I was about to be dipped into the hive.

"I'm not afraid," I said. "But we don't belong. "We're … we're—"

"Losers?" she interrupted.

Maybe, I thought. Right about then my stomach felt like the fat kid that downed the whole bag of Cheetos.

Chapter Seven
Sea and Sand

Curt pulled up at nine o'clock. His car spit exhaust like it was sending Indian smoke signals. Even before I reached the passenger door, Renee had already slipped into the back seat. She wore her customary white t-shirt and jeans even though the night was cool. Curt had on a black cotton skullcap to cover his ears.

"Nice hat," I said before I looked at his feet. "Too bad you didn't lose the shitty boots."

"They're my signature," he explained.

"Yeah, you telling everyone you're a total dick from ten feet away."

He ignored me when the car backfired and nearly drowned out the music pounding from the speakers. My flinch didn't go unnoticed.

"You jumpy, Jimmy?" asked Renee.

"No," I lied. But I didn't say another word all the way to the lake.

Cars were scattered throughout the lakefront neighborhood. The air was thick and a night fog drifted over the trees. The path leading down the slope wasn't marked but we found it without too much problem. A feeling ran down my spine like a melting ice cube but I kept it to myself. Then it magnified when Curt spoke.

"This feels weird. Like I'm entering the Land of the Lost."

"Or Night of the Living Dead," I added. "Just waiting to get devoured by the soulless."

"Mr. and Mrs. Drama," Renee said. "Spare me."

I didn't ask which one she thought I was 'cause I didn't really want to know. I followed both of them and we slid down the hill on our heels and the backs of our hands. I could smell the campfire on the beach. Of course it was illegal to be there, but we were hidden enough that we were probably safe. Probably. Cops were known to make a surprise visit but for the most part if you ran like hell you wouldn't get caught. At least I had the running part covered if it ever came down to that.

We made our way to the group of about thirty or forty kids like we were tied together by a nylon rope. My armpits suddenly turned into water faucets and I wished I was anywhere but there. I was sticking my skinny neck out on the chopping block and knew I couldn't hide from the world forever. Then again, a wimpy voice inside my head said, *Why not?*

The bonfire crackled nearby and mixed with the sound of beer-fueled laughter. The shadows of kids flickered in and out as flames jumped into the black sky. The closer we got to the fire, the more I expected to end up as a stuffed pig roasting on a spit.

"Ready or not, here we come," I said half under my breath.

"Enough already," said Renee as she smoothed the dirt off of her hands. "Let's see how this party rolls."

Curt and I exchanged glances as she moved a few steps away from us. I guessed he felt like I did, but it was too late now. Just like a bungee jumper in mid-air there was no turning back.

We sure weren't greeted with open arms. Open indifference was more like it. I think I got a head nod from a guy or two, but that was about it. At least until I heard a familiar voice.

"Well, I'll be damned," said Rex. "You did come. I made a bet you wouldn't show. I put a buck against you." The glazed look in his eyes promised he was already knee-deep in beer and it was only a matter of time before he was totally shit-faced. "Vance, you see this?"

Vance stepped forward and brushed some hair from his eyes. His lips curled just before he took a slow drink from a plastic cup. "He showed," he said almost as if he was unsure of what to say. "Never would have guessed."

Rex nodded. "Right, hey? And you still owe him for popping you at school, don't you?" He said it like I wasn't even there.

Vance nodded slowly. "Yeah, I do."

I braced for impact but Rex kept on.

"Now he wants in the club? Maybe you ought to beat the shit out of him first. Initiate him."

Then Vance did something I would never have guessed in a million years. He nodded at me. "The beer is back by the oak tree. Help yourself."

I almost fell into the fire face first. I sort of nodded back, but I think it looked more like I was trying to avoid a puff of smoke.

"You Mr. Nice Guy all of a sudden, Vance?" asked Rex. "For real?"

Vance gave me a look that had me confused. Then he shrugged. "No hurry, Rex," he said. "It's still early."

"Whatever," he replied. Then he looked at me. "There are a lot of drunk chicks here. Take your pick. I know I will."

Rex laughed to himself and moved back into the shadows. Then he turned and spun towards another group like a rabid mosquito looking for blood. I took a deep breath and backed away from the flames. It was as if the fire was a thousand degrees and my face burned when I bumped into Renee.

"You okay, Jimmy?" she asked as she braced me up.

I thought for a second. "For now," I replied. "For now." When she touched me I was sure she knew I was totally full of shit.

***

I wasn't a big drinker and I sipped on a beer or two while losing myself among the crowd. Curt wandered and took turns between standing by the fire and skipping rocks into the lake. Renee seemed to be enjoying herself and I caught her throwing back a shot of something. I realized how little I really knew about her and as she talked to people around the fire, I was by myself. It's sucked how alone you could be among a group of people and it was a shitty feeling. Maybe the worst of feelings. When I looked at Curt lazily tossing rocks into Lake Michigan, I felt totally abandoned. Then like a complete wuss, I started to mist over.

"Watcha doing, cowboy?" asked Renee, as she moved next to me. "Riding solo?"

I pretended the smoke was irritating my eyes and rubbed them out. When they cleared, it was obviously Renee was catching up to the rest of the party. I had seen kids wasted before, so it wasn't totally new to me. With the fire as a background, half of her face took on a supernatural glow while the other remained hidden in the dark. I could smell the alcohol on her breath as we sat down in the sand.

"I'm a lone wolf," I said, trying to create an edge of coolness.

"You having any fun?" she asked. "So far most of the kids are okay."

She drank in the last of her cup and tossed it towards her feet.

"You a drinker?" I asked.

"Some. If it's around." She stopped talking and the light of the fire lit up her face. "Sometimes it makes me feel better." She paused and looked out at the water. "Sometimes not."

"Not?"

She shrugged. "Sometimes I think I got it all figured out. Other times …"

"What?"

96

"Other times not so much." She looked at me as if she was measuring me for trustworthiness. I—"

"I heard you were here but I didn't believe it," said a slurred voice from behind us.

We turned to face Veronica and it was all I could do not to swallow my tongue. Renee did just about the opposite and a big smile hit her face.

"I knew I'd see you here, Veronica. I was hoping we could hang together."

"Like that will happen," she said. Then she looked larger when two junior Beez settled at her side. "This is the one I was telling you about. See what I mean?" They nodded together.

"What does that mean?" Renee asked.

"Really," I added weakly.

She looked at me like I was a major nose zit on prom night. Besides Mrs. Spoon's class I had never really spoken to her and at the moment I was glad my voice didn't squeak like a little mouse. She was a total bitch but *damn* she looked good. Her hair and blue eyes lit up like neon in the light of the bonfire. Her black on black outfit rocked and gave her the appearance of a movie star just waiting for the red carpet to be rolled out. But the only thing ready to get rolled over was me.

"You're that guy from school," she said with a major league slur.

I gulped down a hairball that suddenly found its way to the back of my throat.

"Yes, Jimmy Parker," I repeated as if I was trying to convince myself.

"Oh yeah," she said. "The skinny guy that whacked Vance."

Screw you, bitch, I almost said aloud. Then I settled for something a little lighter. "That's me." I stopped talking when she moved closer to get a better look.

Lucky for me, Renee stepped right in. "Jimmy and I were talking, Veronica," she said as they rubbed shoulders. "Is there something you want? Makeover advice? Hair? Anything?" This caused Veronica's small posse to titter like a pair of munchkins from the *Wizard of Oz*. So Renee spoke again. "Do Miley and Cyrus think that's funny?"

Veronica unconsciously smoothed her hair and steadied herself in the sand. "Oh, I'm sure they do. Given that I've done more modeling than anyone in the school I'm sure I don't need advice from you," she said proudly. "Coming that you dress like your clothes are from Walmart."

"Walgreens."

"What?" asked Veronica as she stared at Renee.

"Walgreens. I had a two for one coupon for T-shirts."

Veronica licked her lips and leaned harder against Renee. Then Veronica tried to trump her but she had no idea the contest she had entered into.

"You're really a raggedy-ass little thing aren't you?"

"Maybe, Veronica" Renee agreed. "But I scare the shit out of you don't I? You just can't figure this 'raggedy-ass little thing' out can you? I'm supposed to back down like everyone else and now you don't know what to do, do you? Admit it. You don't know what the hell to do now."

With that Veronica pulled away from Renee and almost fell to the sand. The Beez at her side almost held their breath.

"I have no idea what you mean," Veronica said as she raised a cup to her lips. It was her eyes said something entirely different. She was afraid for one of the first times in years.

"You know exactly what I mean. If you want my advice, it would be to spend less time in front the mirror and actually do something with your life."

That got her angry. A look that said Renee had crossed a line. "Don't push it, bitch. You don't want to mess with me." The munchkins nodded in agreement.

"I'm not looking to mess with anyone, Veronica. I'd just rather you'd go away." She stopped and suddenly looked tired. "Right now I just want to be with my friend." Now it was my turn to nod.

"Good luck with *that,*" she said with a flick of her wrist as if I was a pesky bug. "Have a nice night," she finished with all of the sarcasm she could muster.

"Have a nice night," Renee mimicked and flicked her hand back at the threesome as they disappeared into the night. "Drunk *and* stupid. A special combo."

I was in awe at the confrontation and began to feel a little enthusiasm over the party. That was until a new voice called out to us.

"Hey! What are you guys doing over here?" said some mullet-headed guy I recognized from math class. "We're having a slamming contest. You want in?"

I shook my head and assumed Renee would do the same thing but was wrong. She scrambled up and pulled my hand along with it.

"Why not?" she said. "Jimmy, you in?"

"Uhh, no," I stammered. "I'll watch, I guess."

Renee followed the guy to where the keg was hidden in the woods. I followed reluctantly and kept quiet. A stockade of people was already there and the voices were rising.

"Suck it down!" shouted somebody as somebody slammed back a beer. Rex and Vance were front and center and I stiffened involuntarily when Vance looked at me. Maybe he was surprised I was still there. To tell the truth, I was.

"Who's next?" somebody shouted.

Renee stepped forward to a drunken cheer from the crowd. I shrugged my shoulders at Curt as he stood on the opposite side. I'm sure most of them didn't even know who she was, but anybody willing to suck down a bellyful of beer was more than welcome.

"Get a load of this," Rex said when Renee picked up the tapper.

I wanted to pull her away but stayed silent. *She's a big girl*, I thought. But deep down I knew we were both making the wrong decision.

She lifted the long, black hose toward her lips and tipped her head back. When she swallowed the crowd got louder.

The chant of "chug, chug, chug" was interspersed with clapping. She pounded down enough to get the crowd amped up and only stopped when a burst of foam exploded from her lips.

"Jeez!" said somebody from behind me, "She drinks like a big dog."

Right then I knew Renee's destiny was set firmly in place.

"How'd I do?" she asked wiping her mouth on the back of her forearm.

I could only shrug. "Good I guess. So far you're winning."

"Winning?"

"Most beer per body weight," I said.

She smiled. "I like a good challenge," she replied. "Always have."

Then a new challenge came front and center when Veronica pushed her way to the tap.

"My turn," she called as the crowd parted like the Red Sea. "That was nothing."

Her little bodyguards swayed in rhythm and I waited to see if they would start a cheer. Veronica lurched and made her way forward. The shine of the bonfire lit her hair and with a practiced ease raised the tap to her lips. When the beer began to flow all I could do was shake my head in wonder. *Crazy shit,* I almost said aloud. Veronica gulped the beer down like she was stranded in the desert and had stumbled on an oasis. When the foam spurted from her lips she drenched the closest Billy waiting for his turn at the tap.

"That's how you do it," Veronica said loud enough to let everyone know the intended target.

"What a piece of work," Renee said as Veronica was swallowed up by the crowd.

I nodded to agree with her and studied Veronica's unsteady body. But a part of me south of the border had other ideas.

***

I watched a few more kids take a stab at liquid immortality. Nearby Rex and another Billy took notice of Renee and checked her out high and low. I could tell they liked what they saw when they whispered in each other's ears. Even in the dark, I could see Rex lick his lips as if his appetite had been whetted. When he moved forward, the hair on the back of my neck stood tall. Renee leaned against me and steadied herself.

"Here comes the big bad wolf," she whispered. "Ready to huff and puff."

She was right. Still, something in her voice seemed to welcome the advance.

"That was pretty impressive," Rex said as he stepped between us. "I never would have guessed you could pound it down like that."

"I was thirsty," she replied.

"I'll say. Way more than most girls. Except for Veronica." He winked at me as if he was giving me a go-ahead.

I didn't reply. Me and Veronica. He may have as well said I was going to be the new all-state varsity quarterback. When he pressed in tighter heat came off him in waves. Enough that I took a step to the side to avoid contact but that only enabled him to move closer to Renee.

"You want to check out the fire?" he asked her.

It was only a few seconds before she answered but it seemed like minutes. I waited … maybe I hoped … for a glorious comeback that would cut the asshole off at the knees. It never came. Instead, with a look somewhere between a smirk and curiosity, she took a tentative step toward the flames. When Rex steadied her as she stumbled in the sand, they both laughed. I was in the minority but at that moment I didn't find it funny at all. And in spite of the warmth from the fire, I shivered.

***

I wandered around the edge of the party for the next hour. As the voices got louder, I turned inside myself like a turtle hiding in a shell. When I stumbled over a jagged stone on the beach, I thought of the rock I found that summer. Right then I was just as alone as it had been the day I found it. Renee was nowhere to be found and Curt had undoubtedly poked his nose into conversations that never desired him in the first place. Just as a series of clouds blackened the moonlight, a wall of Billys made their way toward me. Maybe I imagined it, but from somewhere in the distance I heard a cry in the night.

"Hey Vance, he's over here," said a deep voice.

I froze in place and realized I was totally screwed. I considered running but decided I would take whatever was in store. My first guess was that Vance's fist was in the front window.

A group of five blocked any exit and Vance was right in the middle. In spite of my impending doom, I studied him one last time before he beat the crap out of me. He was close to freakin' perfect in a way one guy can admire another without being totally gay. His jaw was carved from stone and he could snap his fingers and have a girl hanging on his arm ready to do whatever he wished. Right then I thought it more than likely Roid-boy was going to break my pointy little chin into multiple pieces.

"I'm just minding my own business," I said weakly. "I don't want any trouble."

"Just like when you hit Vance in the throat?" the same Billy replied. He gulped down the last swallow from a cup before he threw it into the darkness. "Where's Rex? He oughta be here to see this."

"He's with that new chick," said another with a laugh.

Vance remained quiet. Then he spoke. "Why did you hit me?" he said in a flat voice. "I need to know."

People surrounded us but the question was asked as if we were alone on a desert island. I wanted to tell him how at that moment I was sick of my life and he happened to be in front of me. How it wasn't even really about him—that it was about me. Or that maybe deep down even my beat up subconscious was tired of being a loser and just exploded. Unfortunately I didn't say anything even close to that. Instead I just stuttered like a teenage moron.

"I … I … I don't know what happened. I … I … just lost it for a second. I'm s … s … sorry. I didn't mean anything by it."

His eyes narrowed. From behind me I heard something about "kick his ass", but for all I know I could have been imagining it. Then Vance did something strange. He smiled and shook his head. As far as I could tell it wasn't a bogus smile at all. Then he spoke. "Don't do it again."

That was it. Then he took a step back away from the crowd. The Billys rushed him like paparazzi but he pushed them away and walked toward the fire. I stood there for a moment and realized I didn't know much about anything anymore. The waves crashed in from the lake and I wanted to go home. It got even worse a minute later when someone fell in front of me and landed face-up on the sand. I moved to see if they were okay but regretted it instantly.

"Umm," I said as if I was trying to clear my throat.

Veronica was lying on her back on her elbows trying to push herself up. She tilted her head back and showed me the whites of her eyes.

"I fell on my ass," she giggled. "I was looking for a bathroom."

"I don't think there are any on the beach," I said. "Unless you're going to pee in the lake."

"Gross!" she said as she tried to push off the ground "I need help," she admitted. "I'm totally gone."

"That's for sure," I said and leaned over to grab her by her wrists.

The problem was when she pulled I wasn't ready. That made me fall on top of the Queen of the Beez who only days before was a direct threat to my survival in Dweebville. She was spread-eagled and I was suddenly in position to do serious business if a few layers of clothing weren't in the way. Then she did a funny thing. She laughed. A drunken laugh but one nevertheless. But she didn't resist.

"You work fast," she said in a slurred voice. "I never would have guessed."

The trouble was when I tried to get up my toes I slipped in the sand and fell on top of her again. Her chest was as soft as a bag of Stay Puft marshmallows and as much as it felt good, I panicked. I squirmed around like a horny toad desperately trying to get up but the grinding got only worse. Her drunken laugh hit my ear and echoed like the waves from the shore. It only dimmed when a Billy stood over me with eyes ready to explode from his head.

"What the hell?" he said.

Then I think I heard a click but I couldn't be sure.

The screaming began only seconds later.

"The cops!" echoed a shrill voice that caused an avalanche of movement. A pair of flashlights shined from fifty yards away and the combination of light and adrenaline jump-started all of us. I scrambled up and momentarily forgot about my sloppy swap with Veronica. I ran toward Curt and grabbed him by the back of his t-shirt.

"Where's Renee? We have to get out of here!"

"You're all full of sand," he said.

"Never mind," I growled. "We need to find Renee."

"I haven't seen her," he said nervously as he looked toward the lights. "I was hoping you would know."

I looked around the fleeing crowd and caught a glimpse of Rex. I ran towards him and grabbed his forearm.

"Where's Renee?" I asked as the lights closed in.

"Who?" he replied.

"Renee. The girl you were with."

"Is that her name?" he said laughing. "She's back in the woods behind the barrel. Puking her guts out." He pulled his arm away. "She's wasted."

He ran off and Curt followed as I sprinted towards the woods. I stuck my head in the thick brush and called her name.

"Renee! Are you in there?"

I saw a flash of movement and pushed through the bushes. She was sprawled on her side with her T-shirt half-pulled up to show her ribs. She lifted her head and wiped at her mouth.

"Jimmy?"

"Yes, it's me and Curt. We have to leave. Now! The cops are here," I explained in a breathless voice.

"But I'm sick."

"So we heard," I said. I motioned to Curt. "Grab an arm."

We lifted her up like a wounded soldier being carried from the battlefield. There was only one escape. Up. So we each took an arm and started climbing the hill. Luckily there was a small path and even with Curt's stupid boots slipping every few steps, we pushed through the woods. I never would have guessed how hard it would be to make it to the top but it was way better than spending the night at the police station getting bitched at by our parents. I heard shouts from below and guessed more than a few people would end up getting busted. It was sure to be the major topic of conversation at the sophomore pole on Monday.

"I'm gonna puke," Renee said when we finally reached the top of the hill.

She fell to the ground in her mud-stained jeans and T-shirt as she slumped in a heap. I wiped the dirt from my hands on the front of my jeans and tried to hold her up. Then I asked the question that burned for the last hour.

"Why would you go with Rex? I don't get it."

She titled her head back and the streetlights shined on a fifty-cent sized patch of vomit on her sleeve. I almost lost it myself but maintained when her eyes looked away. "No reason not to. When you got nothing, you got nothing to lose."

I had to admit that stopped me in my tracks and Curt looked at me with a confused look.

"What?" I said. "Nothing to lose?"

She opened her eyes wider and looked at me with the same dead look I had seen once before. "You heard me," she said. "Sometimes it's just like, what the fuck, you know? Tonight was one of those nights." She paused. "I know it was wrong to be with Rex. I get that. He's a total prick." She spit something gross toward the ground. "But for a minute I just didn't care. I can't explain it."

I had no answer for that. I had lost count how many times I had done some dumb-ass shit and had no idea why. But I wasn't her. Somehow she was different and I told her so.

"But Rex? He's one of … of—"

"Them?" she interjected. She spit again. "So what does that make us? The good guys?" she asked. "I hardly know who I am in the first place."

I considered the words and looked down toward the lake towards where I fell on Veronica. That moment was long gone, but would forever live in my memory banks. I could still hear a shout or two as the flashlights shined and I wondered who was getting busted. I had no guilt in believing it was better them than us.

"Yes, we are the good guys," I finally said. "We don't step on other people just for fun. We don't look for the weakest and attack like teenage wolves. Rip them up and spit out the bones. We don't destroy someone just because we can. We just don't!" I called into the damp air. I realized I was still holding her up when she looked at me and nodded like she knew something.

"But deep down you wish you were one of them, don't you?"

That stopped me cold and I didn't answer as the streetlight blinded me in the night.

Chapter Eight
Spillover

We barely spoke on the way home from the party. At one point we got stuck behind a train and the dead minutes made me squirm in my seat. I could barely wait for the night to end. We were all like balloons from the state fair tied to the end of wooden sticks slowly losing air and hanging limp. I didn't say a word about grinding on top of Veronica because it just didn't seem like the time - if there ever would be a right time. When Curt dropped me off at home it was in tomb silent and I raised a weak hand to them when they drove away.

That Monday morning I said a few words to Renee but it was obvious she wasn't in much a mood to talk. I didn't force it and hoped things would chill as time went on. She never showed up at lunch so I sat and wasted time with Curt. An hour later I glanced over at her in Mrs. Spoon's class as she scribbled in an open notebook. Then we both looked forward when Mrs. Spoon spoke.

"Good afternoon to all of you," she said. "I trust you all had an enjoyable weekend." I snuck a peek at Veronica but I doubted she even remembered what happened. I wasn't sure if Mrs. Spoon was asking a question or making a statement but it didn't much matter. She spent the next twenty minutes talking about "personification" and how writers used it to get inside of people's heads. "Using characteristics usually attributed to people in describing objects and action," she said. She read famous writers as examples and I listened to their string of words. I read more comic books than great literature and felt stupid about my simple existence. I stiffened when she threw out another assignment to spend the rest of the class on.

"I'd like you to reflect on an event of the weekend and use the personification techniques we've just discussed," she said as a groan filled the room. "It might have to do with something as simple as going to a movie or cutting the grass. Your choice," she explained. "Then I'll pick one of yours to read aloud for discussion during the last five minutes." That really set off the moaning but she was having nothing to do with it. "Please begin now."

I looked at my pen and wished it would magically fill the paper. Maybe it was the adrenaline but in a minute the thoughts jumped out of my brain and covered most of the page. When I was done I tapped my pen nervously and waited. Time went by and I stared blankly hoping to stay as hidden as a booger under the desk. More than once I just wanted to survive the day and today was one of those days. That bubble burst when my name was called from the front of the room.

"Jimmy," said Mrs. Spoon, "why don't you read us what you have written." I almost pissed myself like in grade school but held tight. My heart hammered in my chest as I looked for a place to hide. "There is no right or wrong in the written word," Mrs. Spoon said as she saw me sweating bullets. "If it helps you any, everyone will be reading some of their work to the class this year. You will just pave the way and be done with your part."

That helped a little. A fraction of a little, actually. I bit my tongue and hoped the jolt of pain would stop the shaking overtaking my body. So I read:

An Angry Wind
by
Jimmy Parker

As I climbed down the hill the trees surrounding me screamed in my ear. "Don't do it!" they shouted. "Turn back!" It was too late when I stepped into the sand protecting the earth. My feet sunk and the ground almost swallowed me whole like a ravenous beast. The distant lake pounded and the waves laughed at my very presence. "You don't belong here," they taunted. "Not now. Not ever." The wind whispered like a cackling witch and echoed the same thought. "You're a fool, Jimmy," it called. As it surrounded me and pulled tight, I struggled to escape its bondage. My ribs crushed under the strain and the air was sucked from my lungs. Just as I had been warned, I was an intruder in the midst. Lost and alone. Again.

I set the paper down and stared at it like it was my Last Will and Freakin' Testament. The rustling of the room was interrupted by a sound from the front.

"Hmm," said Mrs. Spoon loud enough for all of us to hear. "Very nice, Jimmy. Class, any comments?" she asked.

I dreaded the next five minutes and felt like a naked convict getting his ass checked for contraband. I cinched up and readied for a probing specially delivered by my classmates.

"I thought it was weird," said Veronica. "Trees can't scream anyways."

Spoon smiled. "You've never heard a whisper in the woods when you've taken a walk?"

"I don't like the woods. Too many bugs." The class split between a shake of their heads or nods of agreement. "What?" she questioned. "The woods suck."

"Be that as it may," said Spoon. "What did you think about the use of personification? Did it work?"

No one else said a word and I was close to blowing chow all over my desk. Then it started.

"I thought it was great," said Renee from across the room. "Nature can talk, you only have to listen." That got an eyeroll from Veronica that caused her posse to titter out a laugh. Renee spoke again. "Veronica, I'm guessing that unless you get a text from Mother Nature herself you would be oblivious to just about everything. Oblivious means you wouldn't notice, by the way."

"I know what it means, bitch," said Veronica in an angry voice. "I know about a lot of things. Like what you and Rex did last weekend. In the woods."

That caused a gasp from the class and Mrs. Spoon stepped in an instant later.

"Enough!" she shouted as she took a step forward. "Veronica, you will see me after class. Understood?"

"Whatever," she replied with a dismissive wave in the air.

But her statement hung in the air like a sick odor and I doubted it would clear quickly. By the angry look on Renee's face, I was right.

***

After a few more comments on my writing the class ended. I gathered up my things and quickly headed for the door. Renee was already half a hallway ahead of me and it was obvious where she was going. The in-between class gathering space was around the sophomore pole in the east end of the school. Every class had an unofficial pole that the most popular hung around whenever they could. Whether it was to show off a new tattoo, a tan, or clothes from the mall, it was the place to been seen or show off, which-ever way you viewed it. When Renee charged through the crowd she might as well have been a one-girl tidal wave.

"Renee!" I called from the distance. Even if she heard me, she didn't slow.

A crowd was already formed around the pole and the Beez and Billys spoke louder than needed. Renee charged in until she found exactly what she was looking for.

"Hey!" she said above the noise of the crowd as she pulled on a shoulder. "Hey!" she said again.

Rex turned slowly and his face registered both surprise and amusement. I would have bet he still couldn't remember her name.

"Yeah?" He looked away and measured the crowd around him. Consciously or not, his chest puffed out another inch.

"What are you telling everyone?" Renee asked him. "You know nothing happened between us, not that you didn't try."

He looked at her and a darkness fell over his face. He wasn't one to mess with and I wished the next few minutes would end before they even began. When he squeezed his right hand over her collarbone it came threateningly close to her throat.

"I said what I wanted," he replied. "That you were drunk and you couldn't get enough of me. I would have given you more but you started puking before I could finish the job." He paused for effect. "You here now to finish things up?" he asked as he moved his hips closer.

Renee turned hard. "You're right, I was drunk," she said in a voice approaching a growl. "Or I never would have been near you. Anyways you wouldn't have been man enough to make it worth my time, drunk or not."

Rex scowled and stiffened as the crowd hooted in reaction. I was on the back edge of the five-deep pack that thickened in response to the ugly vibration.

"You bitch," he said. "You're lucky I wasted my time with you. But that's over. You can go back to the trailer park that you lived in. In Oklahoma, or Nebraska, or wherever." The crowd whooped again and took the confrontation to another level. Renee didn't back down and she took a step closer as her arms rose up toward Rex's face. He caught her wrists and she reddened when he squeezed tight. Then she smiled.

"You going to beat me like your daddy does, Rex? Would that make you feel like a big man?"

He didn't reply as his face hardened. I thought he was going to hit her, but instead he slowly released the grip. He stepped back toward the pole and looked stunned but didn't say a word. Instantly the space he created was replaced by a new entry to the group.

"Why don't you just give it a rest?" asked Veronica. "Nobody gives a shit about what you think or say. So why don't you do as Rex says and take your rummage sale clothes back to wherever you came from. You don't belong here and everyone knows it."

She cut to the quick and most of the crowd laughed at the drama. For once Veronica was right - Renee didn't belong here. Then again, neither did I. Renee proved the point when she charged at Veronica as if she was a middle linebacker on the football team. She hit her in the chest with a shoulder and the air exploded from Veronica's lungs. The crowd erupted and formed a ring around the two combatants as if they were female cage wrestlers. I was deep in the crowd and pushed my way nearer; there was no chance to get close to the action. I had some stupid notion to stop the fight and calm them down but the dual screams quickly pierced that idea. A flail of limbs filled the air and within seconds they were both wrestling on the floor. Renee was on top and she was swinging wildly with a red-faced rage that came from a place only she knew. Then from out of nowhere Mr. Tindel appeared and separated the crowd by simple brute force.

"Knock it off! Stop this now!" he howled in a voice that peeled the walls. He grabbed Renee from behind and pulled her to her feet. Veronica struggled to stand and charged at Renee but Rex held her as he closed his arms around her chest. He nearly lifted her off the ground, but she still tried to kick Renee from the few feet that separated them. She only stopped when Rex whispered something in her ear that only she could hear. I could have sworn a brief smile lit her lips, but it disappeared when Renee kicked back wildly.

"I said enough!" said Mr. Tindel with finality. They both slowed and it was the first time I noticed a smear of blood on Renee's white T-shirt that matched the red of her eyes. Her breathing was frantic and it reminded me of a caged animal trying to break free. Lucky for Veronica, Tin Man's grip held tight until Renee's slowly settled.

"That 'ho' started it," protested Veronica. "Ask anyone."

The crowd murmured in agreement but Tindel was having none of it.

"We'll figure it out later, but not here," he replied. He loosened the grip on Renee and Rex did the same with Veronica. "Both of you walk with me and unless you want a real problem, you will both behave. Is that understood?" Neither answered as they glared at each other. When the warning bell for the next class sounded, the colony of students scattered with a brand new story to tell the rest of the high school tribe.

***

I didn't see Renee the rest of the day but my gut told me she was in a world of hurt. She had started the fight and even though Veronica deserved to get her ass kicked ten times over, it was a major deal when you got into a fight inside the school. I was sure she would be suspended a day or two but that wouldn't be the first or last time for somebody this year. But it was the first time I ever felt even remotely a part of it. Maybe I should have done something more to help, but I didn't know exactly what that should have been.

It was that way for me. I never knew when I should step up and be counted or disappear one more time into the shadows. Most times I stayed in the gray that had become a safe house. It was quiet there and like a newborn in a crib no one would bother me if I stayed silent. But just like a baby another part of me wanted to scream like hell. Still, for the most part I just kept my mouth shut. That was at least, until I had met Renee.

I walked in the hallway towards the locker room and wished I could run away from my problems. I was totally wrong when I was intercepted by shadows twice my size.

"Quite an entertaining day, hey Jimmy?" Vance asked.

"Your friend gets a little jacked up," added Rex. "We like that." He nodded at Vance. "A lot."

I had no real idea what to say. When I got around the Billys I was about an IQ point away from turning into a complete retard.

"She ... she thinks for herself," I said weakly. Then I bit my lip wondering what they wanted.

"We saw the picture of you on top of Veronica." Vance wiped at his lip before he continued. "Tommy got you on his phone. He was very impressed. He said you had it going on. At least until the cops came."

Rex nodded. "We weren't too sure about you. In fact, we thought you were a nark to be honest." He looked to Vance. "Maybe we were wrong."

Vance laughed. "You got ten points already. Veronica's slightly used but she still counts." His eyes narrowed and he took a deep breath before he spoke again. "You said your dad can get us deals on cars? Is that for real?"

"Yes," I said trying to keep my voice strong. "He can." Deep down I had no idea, but I couldn't back out now.

Then Rex took over. "Take a look at the site. We friended you. You can even see your ass on top of Veronica too. You're a JV Gritch."

"At least for now," added Vance. "But you're at the bottom of the point list. You need to go to work." He paused. "Plus your dad needs to come through too."

"I ... I," I stuttered.

"No need to thank us," said Vance. "Welcome to the big leagues."

They both laughed and disappeared into the distance.

***

When I walked home after cross country I headed toward the apartments where Renee lived. I didn't know the exactly where she lived, but figured it was worth trying to find out. The red-bricked complex was over thirty years old and it was where my mom said the "other" people lived. She had said it so often I never even thought twice about what it meant. I understood better when I examined the aged buildings with fading trim and rusted metal railings that framed countless small porches. The complex was massive and I realized I was wasting my time unless I wanted to check each mailbox by name. Luckily it never came down to that when a voice sounded in the distance.

Renee was sitting on a swing in a small park that looked like hell. Park might have been an overstatement—it was actually a tilted metal swing set holding four single swings and an oversized cement tube for little kids to crawl through. She had her back to me and swung on her tiptoes with her head tilting to let the last dying sunrays of the day hit her face. Her eyes were closed and she was singing softly to herself. I walked slowly and listened to her voice:

Looking for a place, with one familiar face
But every day is dark; never seem to find my mark
Like smoke within the wind, blowing cold until it ends
Growing tired in the night, just waiting for the light

"Just waiting for the light, just waiting for the light," she whispered as if it was a private chant to a preoccupied God.

When she stopped, I stepped closer and cleared my throat to help announce my presence. Unfortunately I was such a numnuts I had no idea what to say. So I bumbled out something as best I could.

"Hi … uhh … Renee. I just came by to see how you were doing. I … umm, was just wondering about—"

"What happened?" she said as she saved my stuttering ass.

"Something like that," I replied. "I just wanted to make sure you were okay."

She smiled and pushed the swing with her toes again. "That was nice of you. Really nice."

I think my face turned red. "Yeah, I'm about as nice as they get."

"You really are. It's cool you're here." She swept a hand toward the swing next to her and I took a few steps and climbed aboard.

"I haven't been on one of these in about five years. It takes me back."

"To a better time, doesn't it?"

That made me think. Then I agreed. "For sure," I said.

"Do you see that tube over there?" she asked as she motioned toward the four-foot high cement pipe. "My nephew likes to sit in it and pretend he's in a spaceship flying to outer space. I remember when I was little I sat in one in Salt Lake City and imagined a million things. I look at that tube and it reminds me that was about the last time I was really a kid."

"What did you imagine?"

"That I was on a train or a ship traveling the world. Taking me somewhere. To China or England. Anywhere but where I was at."

"Did it work?"

"As a matter of fact, it did. That little tube is about my best memory of Salt Lake. How sad is that?"

I purposely didn't answer the question. "Being a kid was the best."

"Maybe. Sometimes. Now it just seems a long time ago. Almost like it never happened." She paused. "Part of me wishes I could go back. But I can't."

I nodded my head and agreed and thought of the unused swings in my backyard. "Yes. Things used to be simpler." I pushed off and swung back and forth. "And happier."

The squeak of the metal chains filled the air as they strained under our weight. For a moment neither one of us spoke.

"I got two days suspension," she said quietly. "Veronica got one day. They have a lady counselor that specializes in anger management that I have to go see." She pushed a little harder off of the ground. "I figure I'll go and listen to her bullshit. If she pisses me off I'll just beat the shit out of her." I'm betting my mouth dropped open because she laughed before I even said a word. "I'm kidding, Jimmy. I promise I'll be a good girl."

"You are a pretty good fighter, I have to admit," I said as we swung back and forth. "You wailed on Veronica big time. I doubt she'll be looking for a rematch any time soon."

"No rematch," she said. "I know it's stupid to fight." She kicked harder with her legs and went higher. "But she was really scared. That much I know for sure."

"Scared?"

She shrugged. "I could tell." Then she looked at me as if I didn't have to ask.

"Umm," I said.

Then a second later her bright smile was back. "It did feel really good though! Damn good, actually."

I saw the satisfaction on her face and decided to embellish the best I could. "Gotta get you in the Octagon next. I'll make some money off of you." I pulled back on the metal chains in order to catch up with her. "Direct from the foothills of the Ozark Mountains," I said in the guy's voice that is at every big match. "She weighs one-hundred pounds and possesses a black belt in mud wrestling and eye gouging. As pretty to look at as an Arabian princess, but more deadly than a cobra in heat. She is known for her ribcage splittin', nine-one-one gettin' elbows, and her finger breakin', casket makin' knuckle locks. Please give it up for a newcomer to the ring - Renee, 'The Ozark Amazon', Wizenson!"

She laughed aloud and for a moment everything in the world felt right again.

"You are too funny," she said in a voice that made me believe she meant it. "Thank you for coming. As much as I try not to admit it, sometimes I need a friend."

I liked that she said that. I didn't say anything but felt the same way. We quieted until I spoke again. "Are you worried about Veronica and Rex? I mean that they might do something?"

She nodded no. "I can handle Veronica. I know she'll say things behind my back, but she's not as tough as she seems. Inside she's still just a scared little girl. In our meeting with the principal she wouldn't even look me in the eye."

"Talk can hurt too," I warned. "You know that."

"Maybe." She tilted her head back again and closed her eyes. "But I've met girls like her before. Powerful in a pack but alone they fade faster than perfume from the Dollar Store."

"I wouldn't know about that," I said. "She does run in a damn big pack, though. I'd be careful." I kicked my legs out and tried to get some air before speaking again. It was time to stick my nuts out. "I kind of have something to tell you."

"Kind of?"

"At the party. When you were with Rex."

"Don't remind me," she interrupted. "I'm still embarrassed."

"I know. But when you were gone I kind of … well, I got on top of Veronica. She was drunk and … and I fell on her when I tried to help her stand up. A Billy saw it and thought I was going to town on her." My swinging slowed to a stop. "I'm a Gritch now," I admitted. "Sort of at a cub scout level."

"Holy shit!" she said as she stopped alongside me. "That's crazy. You and Veronica? Holy shit!" she said again.

"Yeah, holy shit," I repeated. "Who woulda guessed?"

"So what's next? I mean what do you get when you're in the club?" She was getting excited now. "Maybe a free feel of any skank you want? Tell me!"

She was way ahead of me and I shook my head. "I have no idea what's next. I haven't even looked at the site yet. I guess they keep stuff there. About how it works."

"Tell me what you find out. Like if that asshole Rex says anything shitty about me." Her dark eyes glistened and she stared straight ahead. "He's really …" She paused.

"Really what?"

"Dark. Maybe even bad. Something about him isn't right."

"Like?"

"He's different than other guys. I've met some assholes before, but he's a whole different breed. The more I talked to him at the party, the more I was afraid of him. Then when he touched me ... well, he was ugly inside. All the way through."

I pushed off slowly and tried to catch her glance. "It will be okay," I promised. "I knew it was a bad idea the moment you left with him at the party. I wanted to stop you."

"It's nice you were going to look out for me. But I don't tend to listen to anyone."

"I hadn't noticed."

She smiled. "Anyways, don't blame yourself."

"I still do, a little."

"Well, don't. At the time, I just didn't care. For once I thought something might work out. I've never had a real boyfriend. Maybe I thought he'd be the first."

"Not him. You're better than that."

"I know that, I guess," she said. "I was hoping I was wrong about him." She paused deep in thought. "It wasn't anything he really said, though. It was just the way he is if you know what I mean. Like being cruel is fun for him." I nodded and waited because it was like she was ready to tell me something she had bottled up for the last few days. "I know I was drunk, so I can only blame myself."

"Blame for what?"

"He wanted more than I would give." When she stopped I couldn't help but glance at the long sleeves that uncharacteristically covered her arms. "I don't know what he would have done if we had been together longer. Lucky for me I almost puked on him." This made her smile. "First time spewing turned out to be a good thing."

"What do you think he would have done?"

"Don't know," she admitted. "I don't want to think about it."

We quieted as the shadows cast a spell over the swingset. The squeak of the chains slowed and the silence was unexpectedly broken when she started into a soft hum. It was almost like a gospel song and she didn't seem self-conscious about letting me hear it. So I asked.

"I've heard you singing," I said bluntly. "Twice now. You do really great. The words are like poetry."

"Twice?" she asked.

I explained about the first time and how I heard her again when I walked up earlier. "You should write them down. Mrs. Spoon would be proud."

She shook her head. "I do it for me and not for anyone else. It helps me deal with things."

"Things?"

"Life," she corrected. Then she studied me as if she was deciding whether to trust me or not. I guess I passed inspection when she kept on. "It's like my brain is different. First it's the touching thing. But it's something else too." She paused again and tried to explain. "I haven't seen my mom for months. Now I'm stuck in a town that doesn't even know I exist. The part of it that does thinks I'm some crazy whore." I wanted to disagree with her, but knew most of her words rang true. "Above that I get …" She stopped in mid-sentence and shook her head in dejection.

"Get what?" I echoed.

She licked her lips and looked at me. Actually she looked more *into* me than anyone had ever done before. Like she was measuring me to see if she could finally trust one person in her life. I only hoped I wouldn't disappoint her when she continued. "I get down, Jimmy. Like really down. It's supposed to be hereditary or some such shit. I guess that's why my mom is so screwed up. When it hits me, it's like the world turns dead and grey."

I barely knew what to say. This girl had some *serious* shit going on. First she's some kind of mind reader and now she tells me she has other issues? I almost wanted to run but no one had ever opened up to me before about something so real. It was like I was

120

an adult for the first time in my life and I didn't know if I was ready. As far as I could tell, growing up sucked. Between paying bills and yelling at kids and bitching at whomever you happened to marry it didn't look overly appealing. Now Renee was pulling me into some serious dealing. The last time somebody totally spilled their guts to me was in middle school when some kid told me he stole ten bucks from the church collection basket and was afraid he was going to hell. That kid I never really cared two shits about, but Renee I did.

"I'm sorry, Renee," I told her. "I mean, I get down too, but …" I left the words hanging in the air.

"But you deal with it," she said finishing up my sentence. "For the most part I can too, but I get so tired sometimes. Some days I can barely move. Like I'm frozen in stone." She bit at the edge of her thumb. "Whatever. Never mind."

I nodded and realized she was telling me her darkest secret and I let the words sink in for a few seconds. Then I replied. "Maybe this new town will be better for you. Like a fresh start."

"You think?" she said almost hopefully.

I nodded silently and that was enough of an answer for her. It was then we both stopped swinging until just the tips of our toes rested in the dirty sand. We stayed that way until a train whistle from the distance broke the silence.

Chapter Nine
The New World

I went to the Gritch site that night. The intro song made me jump when some ex-con rapper blasted out lyrics about "makin' some book wit' my revolver, re-loadin' 'till momma screamin' no mo". It was like I was entering a porn site that like it or not I was now part of.

The site was way beyond bold. Pictures ruled and most of them were of Billys in different phases of drunkeness showing off for the cameras. Shirts were optional and most pictures had some girls hanging on them with their tongue licking whatever they could reach. I recognized a few of their faces, but realized any female was fair game in the plentiful World of Gritch.

Then I saw a section titled "Fresh Jack on Jill" and clicked on it.

And there I was. Spread-eagled on top of Veronica in full view. My skinny ass between her thighs as if she had invited me in for a special party. My face looked as if I was railing on her like a donkey in heat. "Ten points for the rookie," read the caption. "For blue balls minus one!"

I could hardly breathe and wished I had never gone to the damn party. Then I clicked on the next picture.

It was Rex and Renee. They were standing by the fire and Renee was looking straight into the flames. Rex was on one side of her and Vance was on the other acting as horny bookends. Both had their hands cupped just below her ass as if they wanted quick test for freshness. This time it was Rex's turn for h to snake out behind the back of her neck. "Going downtown?" read the caption. Even worse was the "Comments" section. "Crazy bitch wants a boyfriend!!!" attributed to Rex. "Trailer trash wants out of the lot. Who gives a shit? I need points!"

The rest was filled with gravy and dressing from other Billys that urged Rex on to greater action. I felt sick at being even remotely connected to the club. Another part of me wanted to blow it to hell and I knew I needed to get in deeper.

So I hit the keys:

Gotta work harder, Rex. Didn't your coach ever teach you that?

Then I hit enter and leaned back in my chair.

And wondered where the hell my life was taking me.

***

I went downstairs later and as usual my mom and dad were tapping away at their laptops, preparing for the next day. I stopped at the foot of the stairs and took a deep breath before speaking.

"Dad, you have a minute?" I asked.

He looked up over his reading glasses and did a double take before answering.

"Sure. Just one more second," he said as he hit a few more keys. "Gosh darn e-mail will kill me before it's all said and done." His fingers flew for a couple of seconds before he made a big show of hitting one last key. "What's up?"

I cleared my throat loud enough that my mom looked up too. "I need to ask you a favor." They both raised their eyebrows in interest. "I want to send a few guys from school over to the lot to look at cars. Only I … I promised them you would give them a good deal. Is that okay?"

My dad's face lit up like a freakin' Christmas tree with LCD bulbs. He couldn't have been prouder I was sending business his way. "Of course, Jimmy. I'll give them the royal treatment. Treat them like royalty if you want. Whatever it takes."

"I would appreciate it."

He nodded. "They have names, Jimmy?"

I almost said Lucifer and Beelzebub. "Vance and Rex. Maybe some others."

"I'll take care of them. Any friend of yours is a friend of mine."

I stiffened at his words, but didn't disagree.

Chapter Ten
Round Two

I slept like crap that night. The world I had slipped into left me feeling like I was coated in bacteria-filled slime and I didn't know where to step next. I couldn't talk to my parents about it and I even left Curt out of the loop. He noticed it on the walk to school that morning.

"You okay, bro? You seemed spaced out or something."

I didn't think it was that obvious. Curt knew me well enough to read my vibe whether I liked it or not. So I took a chance.

"Did you ever get in over your head, Curt? Like you put your nuts on the table and let someone take a whack at them?"

He almost stopped walking at that.

"No, I generally keep my package in my pants," he replied.

"Curt, I mean it," I urged.

I think he could tell from my voice I was being real. "I've done dumb stuff before. Some things I wasn't too proud of."

"Even you, huh," I asked. "Getting nasty with the babysitter? Or maybe stuck a booger under the pew at church?"

"If you're just going to be a D-bag why should I bother?"

He was right. I was starting to be a douche so easy I worried I was beginning to smell like strawberry. "I'm sorry. I was just being a smart ass."

"I'll say."

"So what did you do about it?" I asked. "How did you fix it?"

"I was really mixed up for awhile and tried to handle it on my own. I even went to confession about it."

"And that helped?"

"Heck, no. The priest made me say three Hail Marys and an Our Father. Turns out later he had a secret willy for little boys. Whatever."

I was confused and shook my head.

He continued. "What I was trying to say was I walked about ten miles that day by myself and finally figured it out. Then I did what I thought was the right thing. Not what someone else told me was right. Somehow, deep inside, I just knew."

I looked straight ahead as the school stood in the distance. I almost took off on a ten mile walk of my own.

***

I avoided contact with everyone that day. I may as well as had duct tape on my mouth for all I said. The Gritch thing had me seriously messed up and I couldn't block it out of my overtaxed brain. Renee's suspension left me on my own so I just drifted through the hallway like a Jimmy the Friendless Ghost. When the seventh hour bell rang to end the day I sighed and trudged ahead.

Two hours later I lined up on the starting line for another race. At first it was the last thing in the world I wanted to do but I re-booted as best I could. I was more than confused that day. In some ways angry as hell over everything. When the starter's gun exploded, I hit it right from the start.

My coach told us that someday we would have a run that would make us feel "omnipotent". He explained it meant "all powerful" or some crap like that. We thought he was nuts and we butchered the word and replaced it with a perverted version that sounded something like "all nipply-filled". Whatever the word, after the first few steps I was feeling pretty damn nipply.

I took off fast and for the first few hundred yards stayed in back in the pack. Most of the guys in front of me were from another school, so I didn't know anything about how fast they were. Then I thought of what Renee said a few days ago about having nothing to lose and flat out took off. I sprinted past a group of guys like they were knee-deep in elephant shit. Once I broke free the voice inside my head pushed me to full tilt and I kept on going. My skinny body had a mind of its own and I pulled away like never before. For the first time in my life I didn't look back to see who was gaining. When I hit the last flag and turned the corner there was only a two hundred yard straightaway ahead. Finally I was going to leave my garbage dump mind behind and come out on top. I hit the jets and was ready for a run to glory when a slight complication arose.

"Go Jimmy!" shouted a strange voice.

The voice came as unexpected as nails on a chalkboard. I turned my head to see my mom's smiling face behind the ropes. I think I mouthed "Mom?" but my spikes caught a slick spot and I fell flat onto my freakin' face. Stone-cold pancaked onto God's green earth in front of about twelve misguided people that cared about the god-forsaken sport. I crab-walked a few feet before getting upright in an attempt to erase the fall. Then I tried to regain my stride while scraping dirt from my sweaty face. The last yards of the race were a blur and I scrambled toward the finish line like a crack-impaired chicken. For the first time ever I made it before anyone else for a first place finish. I caught my breath and got slapped on the back by a few of the varsity guys warming up. When I put my hands on my dirt-covered thighs I spun around and looked for the unlikely intruder.

"Mom?" I said as she made her way towards me. "You're here?"

"Of course," she said as if it was nothing unusual. "You did so wonderful! You beat all the other boys by so much. Even with that, that …"

"Face plant at the end?" I said to complete her thought. "Quite theatrical, hey?"

"Well, I don't know about that, but you run so beautifully!"

I almost said I had been doing well for a while now but let the matter drop. Almost.

"I'm surprised you're here. You haven't come to many of my races." The fact was this was her first.

This stopped her smile for a second. "One of my client's boys is on the team with you. Rob or Bob, something like that."

"Probably Rob," I said. "He's a senior on varsity."

"Anyways, she said that her son said you were doing well."

"He said that?"

"Yes. That you would be on varsity soon. That you work really hard."

"I've been doing my best," I admitted. "Maybe it'll pay off."

"I'm sure it will", she said. "Just like when I'm at work. I keep on …" I was ready to roll my eyes when she stopped in midsentence. "Never mind about me, right now it's about you."

She looked at me with a pride in her eyes I had never seen before. As I stared back the word "stupefied" took its rightful place inside my head somewhere near its nipply companion.

***

The days Renee served out her detention I felt slightly naked. I wasn't exactly afraid of the Billys, but I was intimidated at the very least. Hell, half of them were *shaving* while I was still hoping for my first true whisker to make a brief appearance. I sat at the lunch table with Curt and a couple of goobers he knew from debate. That in itself was social suicide because by pure association I was a soldier in their close-knit Gooberville army.

The Billy patrol was on the move and they made their way closer. I was so used to receiving abuse that I had a hard time expecting anything else. So when they saddled up next to me even Curt's eyes glowed like a Halloween pumpkin.

"Jimmy," said Vance. "I wanted to say thanks."

I swallowed and waited for the punch line.

"What did I do?" I asked.

"You came through. Your dad gave me a good deal on a Mazda. Guaranteed it too."

I knew about my dad's guarantees. It was guaranteed he would smile at you until you pulled out of the lot. Then he would do a little jig until the next fish swam into his pond and nibbled the rust off his cars.

"I ... I hope you like it."

"I'm looking too," added Rex. "If my old man will fork over some money when he gets back."

Then Rex put a sharp paw on my shoulders. "We got a little Gritch convention at my house after the game on Friday. You might even get a chance to gain a few more points and get out of last place. Veronica will be there." He laughed. "Interested?"

I looked at Curt and my mouth puckered open like one of my dad's beloved car buying fish. I swallowed the bait.

"Yeah," I mumbled. "Maybe. Sounds good, I guess," I said it all so fast I was sure it came out as confused as I felt.

"Then it's a definite sort of," Vance said with a laugh.

"Bring your drink of choice," added Rex as his eyes narrowed. Then he added almost in afterthought. "I'd invite your little friend too, but she seems a little nuts."

"Sometimes that's a good thing," said Vance.

Rex squeezed my shoulder harder. "Tell you what. If she promises to behave she can come." He shrugged and released his grip. "Even if she starts some shit in my house it wouldn't be the first time. Or the last."

"I'll see," I mumbled as they moved away from the table. Curt just stared at me like the goober that I truly was.

***

That day guys and girls were split in gym class so the lunch hour was the first time I would get to talk to Renee. She got less than a standing ovation when she headed towards our table. A few kids pointed at her and the buzz in the lunchroom escalated a few decibels. True to form she slid in across from me and looked as if nothing had happened. My guess she had been through worse in her life and the two days was no more than a minor slap on the wrist.

"So hey!" she said in a bright voice.

"Hey yourself," Curt and I said in near unison.

"So what did I miss? National Wear a Thong to School Day or maybe a pep rally for the Cross-dressing Chess Club?"

I choked on my ham sandwich and tried to match wits with her.

"No, nothing as big as that. We heard that for Homecoming the sophomore float is going to go totally green. The rumor is that instead of crepe paper we're going to use secondhand clothes from Goodwill. The cheerleaders are going to collect used iPods and donate them to the homeless. Our theme is 'Keep Greendale Green—And the Homeless Rocking!'"

"Nyu-uh," protested Curt. "I didn't hear that."

"Sure," I said, "Even the poor and destitute should have a little sumpin' sumpin' to put them to sleep at night. I'm all for it."

"I'm glad I missed the meeting," said Renee as she played along. "It's nice the school is so socially conscious."

"True trailblazers," I added with a nod of my head.

"Anything else?" she asked.

"I got another A in chemistry," Curt added. "I might get to be in the traveling Science Club if I keep it up. They got to travel to Des Moines last week for a competition."

"I bet they are a bunch of wild and crazy dudes. Probably scrape the gunk off their teeth and culture it in a Petri dish. The guy with the most fungus wins."

"You're just jealous," Curt said. Then he paused and looked at me. "Why you always got to make fun of me?"

I didn't know what to say to that. He was right; I gave him a lot of crap. Maybe because it was the sheer fact that I could was all the reason I needed. But at the moment it made me feel like a tiny shitball.

"You're right, Curt," I admitted. "It's cool that you're so smart." I almost added that chicks dig the guy with the big calculator, but held my tongue.

"You should be proud of yourself, Curt," added Renee to smooth things over. "Once I was in a science contest and tried to make a volcano that would shoot hot lava. Unfortunately, my mashed potato volcano exploded when the Hershey's chocolate lava overheated. Blasted half the class with chocolate taters. I got a C minus for my 'reckless use of food products'."

"I bet I could iron out the kinks in that one," Curt said thoughtfully.

"I bet you could," she agreed. "Next time I'll call you. Then she turned her attention to me. "Anything new on your part, Jimmy?"

I still hadn't quite come to grasp the fact that my mom made it to one of my meets, so I added that story to the mix. I explained how weird it was to see her there and Renee listened until I was finished.

"Confusing, huh?"

"Totally," I said. "Now she wants to come to all of them. I'll probably have a coronary at the finish line if my dad comes too."

"Take what you can get," she advised. "I would."

I knew I was on thin ice but decided to skate on.

"Do you ever hear from your mom, Renee? Has she called you lately?"

She took no offense and answered as she reached for the customary apple in her backpack. "I haven't talked to her since I got here. I guess she called last week when I was in school and talked to my aunt. Apparently she's living in North Dakota with some trucker. She spends half the week on the road with him and sleeps in the back of the cab." She bit around a soft spot on her apple. "She said if things work out with him, we'd have a place. She also said she'll come by when they are near the area." She chewed slowly and swallowed. "I can't wait."

I looked as her face became hard. "You miss her, don't you?"

She looked out the windows. "Sometimes. But other times living with her was like wearing a chain that kept me penned in. Like a dog in the backyard. Other times it was like *I* was the mother helping her deal with all of her problems." She paused and nibbled again. "It got old acting old if you know what I mean."

I did and I didn't. I knew my parents might be messed up, but to them I was always the baby. Sometimes it pissed me off but sometimes I played it for all it was worth to get what I wanted. I felt a little ashamed, but couldn't undo the past. Just as much as Renee couldn't change the role reversal with her mother.

"That had to suck," I said. "It's hard enough just growing up … with … without having to help someone else do the same thing."

"What are you gonna do about it?" she said with a shrug. She looked at Curt and neither one of us had an answer so she continued. "Well, maybe my mom's latest love will be a prince and take us away to live in paradise. Then I'll be a little princess. Whoo-hoo!" she said and spun a finger in the air.

"You can only wish," said Curt. "Gotta have dreams, right?"

Renee smiled as the hum of the lunchroom added an electrical fiber to air. "You're a positive person, aren't you Curt?"

He wiped at the corners of his mouth to clear away any slime. "I guess I am. Is that bad?"

"Not at all," she replied. "In fact, it's a gift I wish I had."

"Maybe someday," he said. "Things can change."

I liked Curt right then and realized I never gave him enough credit. Deep down maybe I hoped I could become more like him. Minus the pussified boots.

"I have to go guys," he said. "Science Club meeting."

"Of course," I said. "Go change the world, Curt." He gave me a weird look and blinked, but didn't say a word. I turned back to Renee as she looked into the distance.

"I bet it's been the same here forever."

"I don't get you," I said.

"The same. The ones that rule the hallways and the other ones lucky enough to just breathe the air." She looked at me. "You getting enough air?"

I had no answer. Instead I blurted out what was on my mind.

"We've been invited to a party. At Rex's house." She took a bite of apple then set it down on the table. "Vance and Rex came by when you were gone." I parceled out my words like they were in a measuring cup. "I'm sort of in the club full time, I guess."

"Sort of?"

"When I fell on top of Veronica somebody got a picture of us."

She almost spit out the chunk of apple. "A picture when you were on top of her? Jesus Christ! What does it look like?"

"Like a skinny guy on top of a drunk chick." I wanted to add that she had a chest like a mountain of vanilla pudding but settled on a shrug. "It was really quick." I shrugged. "It got me an invite to another party. And one for you."

Her lips tightened and she looked over the room toward The Hot Table. Veronica was smoothing her hair like she did about a thousand times a day. Then Renee smiled in a way that screwed me deeper into my seat.

"Count me in," she said. "I'm a glutton for punishment."

I didn't disagree.

Chapter Eleven
And Stogies for All

Friday night came and I nervously readied for entrance into the forbidden Land of Gritch. Perhaps that's overly dramatic, but I hadn't been able to take a normal dump for two days and was more a pawn in my own life than ever. Even more I hoped to avoid being checkmated before hitting my sixteenth birthday.

I met Renee on the swings outside her place. I waved and she almost jumped off the swing in mid-air. She placed her hand near her front pocket as if she hurt herself. I was more than a little bit off.

"I brought a little treat for us," she said and patted the top of a slim bottle sticking out from her pocket. "From my aunt's liquor collection." She eyed me closely. "She won't even miss it."

She misread my look. "I'm not worried about your aunt and her weekend buzz," I said. "I just don't know that we need alcohol. Especially after last time."

She stared me down. "You wouldn't want to go empty handed, would you? Be a social leper?"

"I *am* a leper!" I said. "That's the whole problem."

She shrugged. "So we go in and see what's going on. We can leave any time if you want. I promise. Just give me a sign."

"Fine. I'll stick my finger down my throat. The universal bulimic sign for 'this place is making me sick'."

"That'll be as good as any." She paused and secured the bottle one last time. "Gritch central, here we come."

I walked next to her in dead silence.

***

Some gangster rapper was blasting from the front door and the bass nearly shook the foundation. My heart beat faster and my lips turned to chalk. I licked at them as we stepped toward the front door. I almost started to knock but Renee grabbed my hand.

"No," she said simply. "Just go in."

I did as I was told. What took me by surprise was the place itself. In short, it looked like a combat zone for suburban refugees. I was used to my home filled with prime cut furniture and this was rummage sale heaven all the way. Mismatched furniture was strewn about the front room as if it had been mixed up in a windstorm. A few pictures were on the walls but as far as I could tell they were hung as if a set of darts earmarked their locations. I stopped walking when two oversized labs barked at us like we were intruders.

"Charles. Barkley. Quiet!" yelled Rex as he turned the corner. The dogs did as they were told and retreated from the hallway. He eyed us and stayed quiet for a few seconds. "You came. Both of you."

I almost reminded him he had invited us but Renee took over.

"A peace offering," she said as she pulled out the bottle from her jeans. "Okay?"

When his smile reappeared I knew Renee had hit a home run and that Rex's booze cruise had already left port.

"Fine," he said as he eyed her suspiciously. "Just don't go off on me again. I'm used to it on the field, but at least then I have a helmet on." He laughed with a deep voice that I hoped to achieve in a few years. "I'll add the liquor to the wop in the kitchen. I doubt anyone will mind." He tilted his head to an open doorway.

"C'mon, I'll show you the way."

We followed like he was leading us to the Promised Land of Alcoholic Youth and Pot Smoking Stoners. Most of the party was in the backyard where groups of kids were scattered in all directions. The wop was in some mini-garbage can lined by a white plastic liner that was nearly overflowing. That didn't stop him from unscrewing the cover and adding in Renee's contribution.

"Time to get it going on," he said as he stirred the container with his index finger before placing it in his mouth. "Finger-lickin' good," he added. He then picked up three plastic cups and dipped them in the drink. The red liquid sloshed over the edges and he nearly spilled them on Renee's white t-shirt. "Drink up," he said. "There's more where that comes from."

They both drained their glasses and I was already a step behind. Then I gave in. *What the hell,* I thought. I took a swallow and the taste of Hawaiian Punch hit my throat first. It was followed by a blast of gasoline that took my breath away. My eyes watered but my ego made me finish what I started. I set the cup down I was officially in. But what I was in, was the question. Rex filled my cup almost as soon as it hit the table.

"Good job, Jimmy boy," he said. "You got some catching up to do."

He reached for the cup and scooped out a refill. I could've, maybe I should've, said no, but I didn't. The fact was at that moment I wanted to blend in with everyone else. Even if it was with some people I knew deep down were the worst kind of assholes.

"Okay," I said lamely.

Renee watched me take the cup from his hand and I felt like Adam eating the apple in the garden. She touched me on the shoulder and a few seconds later spoke.

"It'll be okay. It's no big thing."

I shivered and moved to the side. "Hands off, Renee. And leave my head alone."

She looked hurt. "I didn't do anything. I could just tell. Sometimes friends just know, you know?"

I had no answer to that. At that instant I felt like I was at a masquerade party two weeks in a row. In baseball terms I was leading too far off base just waiting to be picked off. When she lifted her cup to her lips I did the same thing. This time it went down easier and my body warmed a few degrees. Soon a tiny smile lit my face that I had no control over. I was a featherweight and I knew it. When more alcohol hit my system it was like my surge protector blew out and my anxiety was muted to the point I could barely detect it. With God as my witness it felt good.

"Let's go out back," said Rex. "Most people are out there."

I followed behind both of them like a little puppy. I was getting my first buzz on and the world was brighter as each molecule of wop soaked into my brain. I smiled again until a large hand covered my shoulder.

"Surprised you came," said Vance as he squeezed close to the point of pain. "I saw you with Rex so I know you've been taken care of." Renee was only a few steps away. "So you brought your friend. Just keep her on a leash and control her temper." He looked over her at a crowd of girls. "A lot of girls here tonight, Jimmy. Just be careful. Strange things can happen. Wop does funny things." He face had a little shine and glowed in the spotlight lighting up the backyard. Then he slowly released his grip and moved towards Renee. "Hey," he said to her as he held his hands in the air as if to show her he was unarmed. "Peace?"

I could tell she was uncomfortable, but she answered calmly. "Whatever," she replied dismissively. "I just came to hang out. Isn't that okay?"

"Yes," he said in a surprisingly clear voice. "We don't need any trouble. Coach said he doesn't want any more trouble. Right Rex?"

Rex returned his attention to us and scowled at the words. Vance didn't say what he meant, but I suspected Rex was on Shit Street with his coach and had to behave until the season was over.

He ignored Vance and walked back toward the kitchen and almost growled. "We need more to drink. This ain't no pussy party."

I guessed he believed that made up for Vance dissing him in front of us. When he headed off Renee whispered to me.

"Don't forget your secret mission," she said softly.

"Remind me again," I said. "I forget."

She got closer and I could smell the apple scent of her hair. Coupled with the wop the world spun a little faster.

"Search and destroy," she whispered in my ear. "The Gritch is all around us."

The trouble was I was feeling more comfortable all the time. When some dude with a five o'clock shadow handed me another cup I took it like it was an offering from the fountain of wasted youth. I swallowed again and felt better ounce by ounce. Even though I was in the belly of the beast I was more than warm and fuzzy. Then I heard a sound like nails on a chalkboard.

"Well, well. If it's not the Queen and her little court."

"Veronica," said Renee in a flat voice. "I was counting the minutes."

"I bet," she answered, as a host of her cling-ons hovered nearby. She measured up her adversary. "You're not going to go psycho again, are you? Now that I have a fight on my record my dad said it will be harder to get into a college. Not that it will matter to you."

Renee dug her heels in. "Maybe with good behavior and community service you'll get it erased. Just keep your nose clean."

"Whatever," said Veronica.

Then I had an idea, and I threw it out there to see if it would stick.

"Renee, why don't you do that magic trick with Veronica. The one where you touch her forehead and read her mind. That's a cool one."

Renee licked her lips and smiled at me. I knew she was all in.

"That's up to Veronica. But I bet she's afraid."

Veronica looked at her tribe of Beez before she got brave. *Atta girl*, I thought. Then she stepped right into our trap.

"I'm so sure," she said. "Like you can really do that."

"Let's try," Renee said. "What do you have to lose?" Then she slowly raised her hand and stuck out her index finger. She moved it toward Veronica's forehead like she was an evil witch and just before she reached her target she stopped. "Are you sure, Veronica? Last chance to run."

Veronica looked confused and blinked. After a breathe she steadied herself. "This is so lame," she said. "Just do your stupid trick."

Renee touched her on the forehead and Veronica's eyes got wide. I was locked in place and I could have sworn the floor beneath my feet buzzed. Then Renee spoke soft and slow.

"Think of a number," she asked.

Veronica didn't say a word.

"Ten it is," she said as Veronica flinched. "A color?" Veronica leaned back but Renee's finger kept contact. "Vanilla is not a color, Veronica. It's a flavor." Veronica pulled away but she was trapped by the Beez behind her and Renee kept at it. "You get tired of always being in the front, don't you Veronica? The perfect hair and face and clothes. And you've been gaining weight no matter how little you eat. Even worse no boy has asked you out in the last month and you have no idea why. Now some new girl is in town and she doesn't seem to know her place and you just can't figure her out. Worst of all is you feel like you are losing control of everything and no one seems to care." Renee pulled her finger back. "I'm so sorry, Veronica. Really I am."

My spine shivered because I knew it was all true. Veronica stood still and couldn't even swallow. Her face whitened and it was as if she had crumbled right in front of my eyes. But she recovered as fast as she could.

"No," she said in a puffed voiced. "Nothing like that."

I knew Renee was dead-on. Then for a second I was sorry I had started the whole game.

Veronica narrowed her eyes. The Beez behind her waited for her to take control like she had done so many times before and she didn't disappoint. "Totally wrong," she lied. "I don't really know where you came from, but I don't like you. I just wanted you to know that."

Renee suddenly looked older than her years. Tired too. Maybe even closer to exhausted. "Do you think I really need you to like me? Like the world will spin out of control if you don't? Because I honestly and truly don't care." She shook her head. "If you don't get that so sad for you." She looked at me. "Now if you don't mind, maybe you can leave us alone. Jimmy and I have some drinking to do."

Then she grabbed my hand and we walked toward a picnic table covered with cups and a half-filled pitcher. I worried about Veronica for about half a second, but then moved on. I suddenly wondered why we were here and knew we fit in as well as a fart at the prom. Actually I knew we would never fit in. Maybe we would be better off if we never did. Maybe the second level seats were as good as it would get. Then a thought hit me: maybe that was okay.

We sat down and I told Renee I wished we hadn't come. How I wasn't some kick-ass superhero that could break down the walls covered with Gritch graffiti. How at the moment I didn't even care.

"So what do we do?" she asked.

"We toast our futures living in the edges of the darkness. Away from the headliners."

"We just give in?"

"No. We just wait for our opening until someday we'll get in the game. Then crush one over the fence when they least expect it."

"You're a dreamer, Jimmy."

"Here's to dreams," I said as I lifted my cup up in a toast. We drank it down and Renee filled it again. As my brain swirled I didn't mind one bit.

I woke up fully clothed in my own bed, but had no idea how I had gotten there. I had grass stains on my knees and to put it bluntly, I smelled like hell. My mouth tasted like dirt and the jack-hammer in my head pounded like the freakin' Liberty Bell. It took only a few seconds more before I ran to the bathroom and heaved my guts into the toilet. The snot dripped from my nose and as my eyes watered I wished for a quick end to my misery. I had never been hung-over before and at the moment it didn't seem particularly heroic. In fact it downright sucked. I flushed before looking in the mirror and saw my own death-mask with dried spit on my cheeks and hair spiraled completely out of control. Then a memory hit full-on.

It was of Renee.

How after finishing another pitcher of wop we found our way to the edge of the yard and sat against a fence. How at first we laughed at Veronica and everybody and everything that we could see and think of. That alcohol was the main conductor and as passengers we hung on for the ride. Then how she got sadder as the night went on and she told me about the crap in her life. The drifting that left her feeling as rudderless as a broken rowboat in a scuz-filled pond. Then how she dipped her head and became silent. Of how I reached over and put my arm around her as we leaned against that wooden fence. How she looked me in the eyes until I moved my lips closer to hers. Then how they met and I spun like I was on a Ferris wheel as a kid. Flying at unknown heights I could only dream of. But it was better than that. Way better. I remembered reaching out and touching parts I only imagined one day I would.

A door slammed from a floor away and shocked me from my trance.

I looked into the mirror to make sure I was still me.

***

I went back to bed but couldn't sleep. Memories of the night were like a broken mirror with jagged pieces reflecting images in all directions. *What the hell did I do?* That single question kept running through my head. Hooking up with Renee? Was I freaking nuts? *Yes,* replied the creature in a mocking voice, *and apparently a horny one at that.* For the most part I remembered rolling around with her in the dirt and pawing at each other like a pair of stray dogs in heat. At least I didn't think it went any further, because I think I would have remembered *that.*

But now what? Were we like a couple? Should I call her? Go to her house? But then what? Find out she was embarrassed by what happened? So I did the next best thing.

I did nothing. Well at least close to nothing. I made my way to the computer and scanned the usual sites. Then I hit on a favorite I labeled "The Great Unknown" and waited for the air to come back into my lungs. My picture was front and center. Check that. *We* were front and center. Renee and I. Except I was damn near on top of her with my tongue investigating something deep within her throat. Worse than the picture was the caption below it:

He shoots. He scores! Twenty more points for the rookie!

Then I turned it off and went to throw up again.

Chapter Twelve
Aftermath

I walked two hours on Sunday to help clear my head. The day after the party I laid in bed most of the day and pretended I didn't feel good. That wasn't exactly a lie if you really boiled it down. Partly it was to escape my first hangover, but it was also to hide from the thoughts that bounced around like flies buzzing around a dead carcass.

The walk did little good. At first I veered toward the lake, but then decided it might depress me. So I went by the high school but that was an even worse choice. It was totally paranoid but I worried I would see someone who had watched me and my wop-soaked brain grinding on Renee. Eventually I made my way toward her apartment but I didn't see her anywhere. Somehow I thought there might be a karmic moment where she would appear and we would talk it out. In the end I was just dreaming again of a moment that would never occur.

***

Monday morning I nearly tip-toed into school. I dreaded the day and purposely got there early and used my locker door as a shield from the world. I hoped the thin metal would be bulletproof from the ammunition I expected to be on the receiving end of sometime soon.

I eventually made my way to the gym locker room that luckily was deserted. I changed quickly before entering the gym and rested my head against the wall. I closed my eyes and wondered where everything was headed. When I opened them again I noticed someone across the gym twisting around like they were having a freakin' slow motion seizure. Then I recognized it was Tin Man. I watched him move for a few minutes until he stopped to suck in the gym air. He closed his eyes and breathed as if each molecule of oxygen was a sacred blessing. When he was done he caught sight of me and nodded. It was only seconds later he was standing over me.

"Tai Chi," he explained. "For the mind and body. Totally relaxing. You ought to try it …" he paused before continuing. "Jimmy. Right?"

I nodded. "Yes, Mr. Tin," I said before I cut myself off.

"It's a whole 'nother world when the stress is gone," he said as he walked away.

I couldn't imagine that world, but nodded as if I understood. Then my shoulders tightened almost on cue when Renee walked in the gym. She looked at me before her eyes flicked around the gym. It was like she was looking for safe spot anywhere somewhere away from me. Then she walked turned and walked my way. My brain did a little dance but I just sat and waited. I tried to look distracted but at best it was a weak attempt to avoid direct eye contact.

"Jimmy," she said plainly.

I nodded like a weak tit. "Hi," I mumbled and attempted to smile.

"Can I sit?"

"'Course," I said with a nod.

"So …," she said as she drew out the word. "Are we going to talk?"

I wanted to talk about as much as I wanted old Dr. Brown to grab my junk and tell me to cough.

"Sure," I finally said but didn't know where to start. So I just dove in the pool and hoped it wouldn't be a belly flop. "I don't remember everything about Saturday," I admitted. "But ... I remember enough."

She smiled. Sort of. "I'm the same. Wop sucks."

"I think the next time I smell Hawaiian Punch I'll chuck on the spot." The joke lightened the mood and she smiled.

"Definitely. But ..."

She left the word "but" hanging in the air. So I latched on to it as best I could.

"I ... it," I said as the words trickled out. "It was just something that happened. I mean ... I liked it ... I think. We don't have to make a big deal of it." I blew out some air and realized I was an inch away from sounding like a pussy. "Unless—"

Renee jumped in. "I think we should just leave it there."

My mouth flew open. "In the dirt," I said without a thought behind it.

"Yeah. In the dirt like two drunken dogs."

I think we both realized it had just happened. Then just like a text sent when you were pissed off there with no way to make it disappear. So we just filed it away for now. Then I remembered.

"They got pictures," I said.

"What? Who?"

"Someone. A Billy. Whoever." I stopped for a second. "They posted us together on the Gritch page. I saw it yesterday."

I wanted to say I was sorry. I wanted to go back in time and delete the party. The moment her face turned red I was at a loss. When the gym doors slammed open and faces appeared we just stared into the distance.

***

We didn't speak again in gym class but I knew Renee was upset. As much as she would say she didn't care what people thought about her, like nearly anyone in school she did. Unfortunately so did I more than I cared to admit. I stayed to myself that morning but my head imagined any whisper was about me and Renee. *Paranoia, thy name is Jimmy*, an unseen voice echoed. It stayed that way until I slunk into the lunchroom and sat with the usual suspects. I would have bet my cell phone that Renee wouldn't show, but I would have lost. She slid into her chair and appeared smaller than normal. I guessed it was one thing to be a "player" for a guy, but for Renee she would get tagged as just another skank available for the make. Only this time I was the one to doing all the dirty work.

"Hey, Renee," said Curt in a cheery voice. "Have a nice weekend?"

She looked at me and considered the question. "It was different, I guess."

"Different?"

"Curt, some other time," I said with an edge I hoped he would notice. He looked at me and gave one of those looks that said "what?" Fortunately he quieted.

That was until a shadow fell over us. Out of nowhere, Rex straddled the chair next to Renee and joined the conversation. He smiled as Vance and another Billy set up court behind her like judge and jury.

"Don't be shy," he urged. "Why don't you tell him about the weekend? About the party. It's a good story."

Renee stared him down and color drained from her face. I swallowed hard and calculated what I could do, but came up empty. She took a short breath and looked up. Then she cut to the chase.

"You mean how I got drunk and messed around with Jimmy? Is that what you want to hear?"

It may have been what Rex wanted, but it was the last thing I needed. Curt eyeballed me but I ignored him. Then Rex leaned in to move closer to her.

"Something like that," he hissed. "Your points helped your boy move up in the ranks. Jimmy's in the top ten for the week."

Her face tightened so much her skin thinned.

"You're a real asshole aren't you Rex?" she said. "I knew it from the first day I met you. I must have been crazy to think differently."

His cracked tooth smile reappeared like a Halloween pumpkin minus the candle. "We'll get together again. I know it."

"Not unless you got a thing for corpses."

It was obvious he liked in-school challenges as much as he liked crushing the opposing quarterback. When he narrowed his eyes my heart beat faster. "You got a mouth on you, don't you?" he said in a low voice. "I like a girl with spunk. Sometimes you just have to learn how to tame a wild child like you."

"Go fuck yourself, Rex. I screwed up but it won't happen again. Ever."

"Oh c'mon. I felt a little something between us." His leering smile said more than words. "I bet you did too."

"I bet it was little. I'll take your word for it."

That gained a gasp as she hit him where he lived. They weren't even touching so this was all Renee without any special insight. I sort of admired her guts, but looked around for teachers in case the need arose. I didn't see anyone close by but caught Vance's eye as he watched the situation. I had no idea what he was thinking and looked back to Rex when he growled out his reply.

"You don't know who you're messing with, do you?" Renee shrugged and fingered an apple in her hand. "I didn't think so. What you need to know is that I usually get what I want, right Vance?" Vance nodded obediently without saying a word. "So remember that," he said and moved close enough to force Renee to back away. "And remember it well, you sleazy bitch."

Renee stiffened and with a screech Rex pushed his chair away from the table. It was only then I noticed Mrs. Spoon watching from the distance. Her already wrinkled brow gained another set of lines as she watched Rex laughing at Renee. But I wasn't laughing at all. Renee was my friend, one of the only ones I had. In spite of our hook-up we were connected deeper than just by flesh. In a few short weeks I knew more about her than ninety-nine percent of the kids in the school. Even with her flaws what I knew I liked. She may have come with a bizarre power and covered with emotional dents that left her far from perfect. I sure as hell knew I wasn't close to being canonized Saint Jimmy anytime soon. As Rex's jackass laugh filled my ears I got angry for the first time in as long as I could remember. Not just pissed off enough to act tough, but full bore balls-to-the-wall angry. Then something strange happened. Maybe it was all the kids watching in the cafeteria. Maybe it was that Renee was across from me looking lost and wounded. Or maybe it was that I was tired of damn near everything in my world. Anyway it was split; I sucked it all in and got more jacked up than ever before. At that instant it was like I left my body to look out from above at the whole messed-up scene. I measured Rex's mocking smile I had seen on a thousand faces before and I cracked. I jumped from my chair to climb on the table and dove straight towards him with my arms extended. The web of both of my hands caught him dead-on his adam's apple and my shoulder struck his collarbone. It popped as if I had opened a soda can right then and there. Rex clutched his throat and retreated a step before his eyes blazed.

"Whaa?" he said an instant before coming back at me.

A punch hit me in the side of the head and it was like a wind chime had been inserted in my skull. I drove at him again and landed a bony shoulder into his gut. If we had been playing Texas Hold'em the announcer would have declared I was all even though I had no chance to win. Surprisingly Rex stumbled back against another row of chairs and one of them clattered to the floor. Some other Billy jumped me from behind and his fist started a warm flow from the back of my head. That got Renee to leap onto a Billys back like a crazed cougar going after its prey. The moment became even more dreamlike when Curt climbed over

the table and charged another random Billy. The noise
escalated and the "fight" chant echoed but I kept driv
ward. I pushed as if it was the starter's gun of a race and I didn
let up. Rex fell into somebody's lunch and sent a pudding snack
flying toward the floor where it left a giant glob of chocolate. He
started to wail on me from all angles but for the most part his
punches bounced off of my arms and my ribs in one piece. We
ended up face-to-face and by the smear of blood on his cheek I
realized he bled red just like me. That was just before everything
went black.

***

I woke up lying on the floor of the cafeteria looking up at the
ceiling, I noticed it was missing a few tiles but of more concern
were the tribal drumbeats pounding in my head. Mrs. Spoon was
kneeling next to me and alongside her was a school cop. I was
screwed, but it was what it was. I tried to sit up but she put a firm
hand on my chest to keep me still.

"Stay down, Jimmy. Not until the nurse checks you out."

I nodded and my head pounded again. "Where's Renee?" I
asked trying to clear my thoughts.

"She's fine," she nodded back. "But …"

"But what?"

She squeezed her lips together. "She's not hurt physically. But
being in two fights is not good."

"But I started it," I admitted. "Rex came over and was giving
Renee shit. So I just, I just—"

"I saw. We both know that still doesn't justify everything." She
touched a tender spot on my forehead. "It will be up to the principal to deal with it."

Then she touched my shoulder and I looked in her eyes. For the
first time I saw her clearly. Knowledge flowed through her and I
wished I had a fraction of her wisdom, but realized it would take

ιne a long time to get there. Ignoring the jackhammer banging in my head, I spoke.

"How do you know, when you know?"

She narrowed her eyes. "I'm afraid I don't understand, Jimmy."

I refocused and tried again. "I mean, when do things start to make sense?" I shook my head slowly. "I try to figure things out, but it never works." I looked her in the eyes and decided to take a plunge. "When do you just feel right about things? When Mrs. Spoon?" I asked desperately.

A sad and slow smile crossed her face. "That is impossible to say, Jimmy." She looked at the students being herded away from the fight. "Some days I wake up and think my place in the world is perfect. Then I see or hear something that confuses and even worse, frightens me. Like right now."

"But I had to stand up for Renee," I explained as everything got misty. "No one else ever has. She's really a good person. I know she is."

"She may be, Jimmy." Then she looked at me as if she was going to start to cry. "It is possible your actions may even be admirable to some extent. But ultimately violence is pointless."

"You think I should have talked to Rex? About what a prick he is and how he hurts people? About how he should change?" I asked. "Like he would understand?"

She shook her head. "No. His type will never understand," she said in an even voice. "I know that. I also know that when you get in the real world fairness is a fairy tale. A myth. What is real is who you are in your inner being. In the depth of your soul. I believe that not all of God's creatures, including Rex, will ever have the ability to grasp the true meaning of life."

"And that is?"

She sighed. "You really want my version? Right now?"

"Yes."

She looked me in the eye. "I believe we need to let the grace of soul grow like a seed from the ground. One that will never stop reaching for the truth however far that may be. So much so, that when you put your head on your pillow at night, you are content that you made a difference in the world. Be it miniscule or enormous."

I considered her words. "Do you sleep well?"

Her eyes burned brightly but somehow she seemed a thousand miles away. "Some days are better than others, Jimmy," she said. "Some days better than others."

***

I didn't face the executioner's squad right then. The school nurse checked me out and after determining that my brain wasn't scrambled eggs, she called my mom. The nurse told me that no one else was really hurt too badly. Rex had a bloody nose and good old Curt had a few scratches on his face. Renee was okay physically, but she was paddling in Shit Creek with only a pair of chopsticks. In other words, she was totally screwed.

My mom arrived within fifteen minutes completely out of breath. She rushed into Nurse Rachet's office as if she expected to find me on a cold slab with a sheet over my head.

"Jimmy, are you okay?" she asked.

"I'm fine, Mom. Just a little headache."

"You were in a fight?" she asked in a high-pitched voice. "Did somebody attack you?"

I shook my head and told her the truth. "No, Mom. I started it." "You?"

"Yes, me." I was actually a little annoyed by the tone of her voice. Like I was too much of a freakin' wimp to ever get into it with anyone. "They were hassling Renee and it wasn't right. So I stood up for her."

"The girl that was at the house? The one that wants to move into a new place with her brothers?"

"Yes. She wasn't doing anything and a few of the Billys came over."

"Billys?"

"A group of guys. One in particular."

"They were hurting her?"

I thought about that and tried to explain it to her. "Yes, but not in the way you think."

"What do you mean?"

"They were making her less than she was. She doesn't have to put up with that." I paused. "No one does."

Then for the second time within the week, my mom caught me totally off-guard. She bent over and whispered in my ear. "You do what you know is right, Jimmy Parker. You'll never regret it as long as you live."

Then I lay back down on the nurse's cot and wondered what planet I was on.

Chapter Thirteen
Bound and Gagged

My meeting with the principal was at eight a.m. the next day. Of course, my mom and dad both had to be there. The night before we spent about an hour talking, which was about fifty-eight minutes longer than I was used to. I explained the situation and they listened. Dad actually even let a phone call go to voice for the first time ever. Things kept getting weirder when my mom said she would cancel a meeting the next morning. She lived for those damn things but this time she said it would have to wait. After that she could have knocked me over with a flick of her rhinestone-encrusted fingernails.

We arrived together in the office and sat quietly. I started to sweat like a fat guy in a sauna and hoped like hell I wouldn't stink up the place. I had never met Principal Scheel before, but he had a rep of being tough but fair. I was sure he had no idea at all who I was when he stood up from behind his desk to shake our hands.

"Good morning, Mr. And Mrs. Parker. And Jimmy," he said with a nod, "I don't believe we have met."

"Umm … no," I said. "We haven't."

"I didn't think so." He paused to open a folder sitting on his desk. "I think we all know why we are here. I have reviewed the report from Mrs. Witherspoon," he said diving right in. "But first Jimmy, I would like your version of the events."

So I told him what happened. I knew I was in the wrong and admitted it. What I didn't tell him was that it felt damn good. I had gotten into it with two Billys already this year and deep down I didn't regret it. At least not yet. One more time, though, and it was probably three strikes yer out. Still, somehow I felt like I had grown a spine for the first time in my life. When I finished my story I sat quietly and took a deep breath and waited. My mom and dad jumped in and told him what a good boy I was, blah, blah, and blah. How I had never gotten into trouble in school before or anything even close. They left out the time in grade school I stuck a wad of bubble gum in some dumbass kid's hair but other than that they came clean. When they finished their begging they sat back in the cushioned chairs and waited.

Mr. Scheel scratched a small scar on his chin and looked tired. I guessed he was worn out from having to deal with crap every day, but I guessed he got paid major bucks to pick up teenage garbage.

"So Jimmy, what do you think I should do?" he finally asked.

I hated when grown-ups did that. Like I would tell him to put my nuts in a vice and clamp down till they exploded. *Do whatever you want!* I felt like screaming at him. It wasn't as if he would do less just because I begged forgiveness or started bawling like a little kindygartner. So I just blurted out the second thing that came to mind.

"I would probably bend me over and give me one hell of a spanking." The moment I said it, I wish I could have sucked it back in. *Where did that come from?* I thought. *What was going on in my head?*

"Jimmy!" said my mom as she sat up in her chair.

I stiffened and tried to back out of my own web.

"I'm sorry, Mr. Scheel. That … that … that was uncalled for," I said as my stuttering double reappeared. "I suppose I deserve a suspension or something."

A painted-on smile re-appeared. "In another era a heck of a spanking might be applicable," he said. "But those good old days are gone." He looked back toward my parents. "Jimmy will have to serve a two day suspension as is noted in the school handbook. The suspension will start today. It is the standard protocol for fighting on the school grounds. In addition to that on those two days you will report to Mrs. Witherspoon's classroom after school to assist her in her work. She tells me that you have a talent in writing and that you are very bright." He rubbed away a fleck of white stuff from the corner of his lips before continuing. "I have yet to see it in our short meeting, but I will trust her judgment on the matter. Is this acceptable to everyone?"

My parents mumbled and bumbled their appreciation for his time and assured him I wouldn't screw up again. I wondered how they could even promise that because I was the only one with any real say in the matter. I held back and gave them my best whipped puppy eyes.

"We are finished then," he said. "Jimmy, on your way out send in the next student in the waiting area."

"Yes sir," Then I stopped just before I reached the doorjamb. "Mr. Scheel," I asked as I turned back, "when you were a kid did you ever wail on somebody if you thought they deserved it?"

My mom gasped, but he didn't miss a beat.

"Jimmy," he said as he rubbed at the scar on his chin again with a distant look in his eyes, "the next student please. Nice meeting you all." Then a small smile crossed his lips.

***

I went home and split the rest of the day between listening to music and sleeping. All in all, for the most part it wasn't a bad gig. Unfortunately, it took a suspension and a future date with Rex's knuckles in order to get it. I wondered where all of this was headed. I wasn't used to conflict and in fact I hated it. I was used to being the one so far from the action that I needed a daily text I was still even in the game. *Maybe I could change*, I thought.

The other half of me knew change was scary as hell. When I sat in my room with the music pounding I was teetering on the edge of a barbwire fence and could go either way. Either direction a hard fall was going to happen sometime soon. I just hoped I could handle the impact.

***

At three o'clock I made my way to school and walked quietly toward Mrs. Spoon's classroom. I beat the final bell and waited for everyone to leave before slipping into her room. No one saw me, or maybe no one really cared. Either way I was happy to get there in one piece. Mrs. Spoon was erasing the blackboard and for the first time I realized how hunched her back was. It was arched like the slice of watermelon and looked like it might hurt like hell, but if it did she never let on. I still thought of her as the most energetic teacher I had but when she turned to face me she just looked old and tired.

"Mrs. Spoon?" I asked in an attempt to get her attention.

She turned and spoke. "Jimmy. Thanks for coming."

I thought that was a weird thing to say. "I'm not sure I had a choice, did I?"

"No, actually you didn't, I suppose." She set the erasers into the tray and took a step toward me. "Are you doing okay?"

A vague question if I ever heard one. *Compared to what?* I thought. To a rat who had just swallowed a mouthful of poison? Or maybe a raccoon caught in a trap clamping down on his hind leg. It was all relative and I told her so. "I'm fine I guess. Doing as well as I can, considering it's the first time I've been suspended."

"Hopefully the last."

"Uh-huh," I agreed. "I hope so too."

She studied me like another assignment ready to be graded. "I was there for the whole episode in the lunchroom. I just got there too late."

I nodded. "I saw you there." I slid into the desk closest to hers. "It just kind of happened. I never expected to do something like that. I mean ... that's not like me."

"I'll admit," she said. "It caught me off guard too. You looked like Spiderman the way you jumped. Quite impressive."

I flushed immediately. I knew she was semi-joking, but I ran with it. "I used my spidey-powers. But only for good, not evil."

She laughed—sort of. "That is debatable. Of course we have a zero tolerance against fighting in the school. By my count that makes it the second confrontation I've seen you have this year. Is that correct?"

I reddened again. "Kind of. The first time was sort of a semi-accident. This time I was angry."

"Angry?"

"Rex came after Renee. And I just lost it." I looked at her. "I know it was wrong, but at the same time it was the right thing to do." I took a deep breath. "I'd do it again."

She took a few steps forward and sat down in the desk beside me. Then she looked at the desktop before licking a finger and rubbing at some graffiti on the surface. "I understand how you felt. Sometimes I would like to take a few heads and knock them together like they were a pair of coconuts. As much as I want to do so, I value my job more. As an adult, I have to act a certain way."

"Act," I said. "Is that all it is?"

She looked toward the blackboard and thought about her answer. "Maybe act is the wrong word. Perhaps I need to say, conduct myself. Growing up is not easy and it is fraught with peril. Yesterday you stepped in a deep pit."

"I did," I agreed. "But high school sucks. Sometimes I really hate it." I caught her nodding at me and changed my statement. "Except for your class of course."

"No sucking up allowed, Jimmy. I've been here many years. Maybe too many years actually." She looked out the windows and seemed to be searching for answers blowing in the wind.

"Too many? What does that mean?"

She looked at me as if she was confiding too much. Then she spoke slowly.

"This will be my last year. I'm retiring."

"Retiring? You?"

"Yes, me. Does that surprise you?"

Well. Most of us think you will be here, well, um ..."

"Forever?"

"Something like that," I admitted. "It's like you're an icon. They'll probably make a statue of you someday."

"So there's a landing place for the pigeons? I'm certainly no icon. That's a heavy burden for anyone." She sighed and massaged her forehead. "Anyways, lately I feel more rusted than shiny. The times are very different now than they used to be. The reality is the students have changed in the last ten years. Definitely not for the better."

"How so?"

She was warming up. "Their lives are no longer about pep rallies and getting their school work in on time. It's more about tan lines, showing off your boxers or thongs. Sometimes even worse," she said vaguely.

"Worse?"

"Don't play dumb, Jimmy. I know you're smarter than that. There is an evil element in this school. Maybe in most high schools these days. I have talked to Principal Scheel about it, but there is little he can do on his own. My fear is it is taking down some of the good kids along the way."

I looked at the walls covered with posters filled with corny messages like "Try writing, you'll like it" and "Just write, you can't go wrong". I turned to Mrs. Spoon and asked her dead-on. "Mr. Scheel said you thought I was okay at writing. Do ... do ... do," I started stuttering again.

"Yes, I do," she said saving me from myself. "You think about the assignment and your brain selects the words to describe what to put on the paper. I liken it to the tumblers on a lock falling into position until the lock opens. You have something that is both rare and special. Raw, but special."

My mouth dropped and I took a deep breath. "I never liked to write before. I thought it was pointless. Now the more I do, the more I want to. It's like you opened a faucet in my head and my sinuses are draining all over the paper."

"Exactly," she said with a smile. "Imagery at its best." She paused. "Fortunately you're not the only one in the class that has impressed me." I waited for her to continue. "Your friend, Renee, has demonstrated some talent. She pours out her heart on the paper. But, she has an unsettling message within her writing."

I thought about some of the things Renee and I talked about since we met. I knew she had troubles. It also didn't surprise me she was good at writing.

"She's become my friend since the day we met. She's different than most." *Way different,* I almost told her.

"Yes," said Spoon. "I see that."

"What is happening to her? I mean with the fight and all?"

"Without getting into specifics, she is getting a full week of school suspension. Because it is her second altercation she must undergo additional counseling. This will be her last chance in this school."

The tone of her voice was dead serious and so was I. "She's a good person, Mrs. Spoon. Maybe she has some problems, but she's not like the other kids. At least not the ones I know."

"How so?"

"She's just more real somehow. More honest."

"Possibly." She looked at me as if she was calculating my trustworthiness before going on. "As a teacher I'm sure you are aware I cannot get into specifics, but her writing is so deep and emotional that I worry where it is coming from. She literally bleeds her heart onto the paper drop by drop. Almost to a degree that it is painful to read. It is apparent she is wise beyond her years."

"She's been through a lot," I said without explaining myself more fully. "You'd be amazed."

"Without knowing a single detail, that is obvious in her writing."

"But she'll be okay. At least I hope so."

Mrs. Spoon narrowed her eyes and the human lasers bore in on me again. "You hope so?"

I stopped to think if I should say anything about Renee's being able to get inside people's heads but knew she would never believe me. Mrs. Spoon would probably have us both see the school shrink and just to make sure we weren't freakin' nuts. Even though Mrs. Spoon was cool she was still a teacher and had to stay on her side of the fence. But I decided I could at least tell her one thing. "She has these … these moments where she's not really herself anymore. She turns into someone else. Like she gets totally depressed. Renee didn't really want to talk about it at the same time that she did. I didn't dig as deep as I probably should have. It was almost as if I didn't really want to know. Like it made me, made me, well—"

"Uncomfortable," Mrs. Spoon chimed in to help fill in the blanks.

"Exactly" I said. "Like it would make me dirty somehow." I paused. "Does that make sense?"

"Yes. Most of us want to avoid things that could be unsettling. A wise man once said 'living is easy with eyes closed'."

"Ghandi?"

"No," she said with a smile. "Compliments of man named Lennon."

"The communist?"

"No, the Beatle."

"Right," I sort of mumbled back.

Mrs. Spoon scrunched her eyes and spoke in a harder voice. "Keep your eyes open and watch out for her. Just like all of us, she may need a guardian angel at her side. Even if you didn't ask for it, I think you've been handed the job."

I nodded and looked out the window as the wind blew the tree branches in the darkening skies.

Chapter Fourteen
Shadows in the Night

I stayed home the next day and spent another few hours in Mrs. Spoon's classroom after school. We talked about books and writers and it was almost like a little electrode blinked in my head. She gave me a book to read and I could barely put it down. Even my mom noticed I was reading something besides some lame comic book.

"I never saw you read a *real* book before," she said in amazement. "I wasn't sure you still could!"

She was joking, I think. As I plowed through *The Catcher in the Rye*, I hardly heard a word she said. I was more into Holden Caulfield and all of his "goddam" problems. He made my crap seem smaller than a cat turd in a kitty litter box.

"I can read," I told her. "I just needed a little direction."

She looked at me as if I was some new space alien suddenly beamed into her home. In some ways, I was.

***

I didn't see Renee at all that week. Each day I walked through the grounds of her apartment complex hoping to find her. More than once I sat on the swings a few minutes before moving on. I was pissed I had never gotten her address but with over a hundred apartments it was hopeless to knock on every door. Just as bad, I didn't know her aunt's last name so I couldn't even check the mailboxes.

That Friday I ran another race and sucked big time. It was like I was stuck in a cloud and couldn't find my way out of it. I ended up about fifteenth in the JV race and even Curt crushed me for the first time. Today he could have beat me wearing his cowboy boots.

"What was up with you?" he asked. "You ran like crap."

"Worse than that. I had nothing," I admitted. "Maybe it was the week and all. I just couldn't move today."

"Understandable," he said. "You've been through a lot. By the way, you got a little rep from the other day."

"What do you mean by that?"

"Word has it that you're a little wacked. In a good way, that is."

"How's that?"

He licked the sweat off his lips. "The talk is that you go off at times. In the future I think people might be less likely to give you any trouble."

How about that, I thought. I show a mental defect and *then* I get respect? "Maybe I should have gone wack a few years earlier," I said. "Still, I don't think I'll be a full-fledged Billy any time soon."

"Thank god for that. Not that you want to be anyways." He suddenly stopped and a serious look crossed his face. "I've also heard that Rex is talking a lot of shit. Mostly about Renee."

That was just what I was afraid of. Actually, I'd bet it's what she was afraid of too. "What is he saying?" I asked.

"Nobody said anything specific. Just stuff like 'Rex is looking for your little girlfriend'. Things like that. Have you seen her at all?"

I shook my head. "No. And I've looked at her complex. I don't know how to find her. It's like she disappeared from the face of the earth."

Curt zipped up the sides of his sweats as we got ready to cool down. "Like a ghost."

I nodded as a cold lake breeze smacked my face and made me shiver.

***

After the bus dropped us off from the race, I decided to walk home instead of ride with Curt. I took the long way home and veered through the apartments. The wind was whipping harder and with the sun setting it was colder than usual. The light poles swayed in the wind and were matched by a few trees already starting to lose their leaves. I pulled my hoodie tighter in order to block the cold and pulled my backpack over my shoulder. The night sky had a strange light and the clouds had an orange glow that reminded me of a Halloween pumpkin. Renee's apartments looked like castles in the distance and I remembered my mom's warning when I was little: "Watch out around there." Back then I was worried there were monsters or kiddie-snatchers or something like that. Now I realized it was poor people that left her feeling threatened for reasons I had yet to uncover. Fear of the unknown, I now assumed.

Maybe it was because her words were rattling around my brain, but when I stepped on a dead branch the crackle made me jump. I gathered myself and marched ahead. There was no one else in sight and I was pretty sure I would come up empty again. A red brake light glowed in the dusk as a car left the parking lot. I got a long look from an old lady in a rusted Ford who probably thought I was a car thief or some punk ready to jack her shitty car. Actually I was just the stalker of a friend that I couldn't find. Or so I thought.

The red burn of a cigarette gave her position away. She was huddled against the side of a building to my left. I couldn't see if it was her for sure but deep down I knew it was. I took a small step forward and a few more twigs snapped under my feet. The wind picked up as if on cue and I called out.

"Renee?"

The glow of the cigarette got brighter. I almost called again but she answered a second later.

"Yes," said the voice.

The word came out soft like the volume from an old radio. I waited for more but when nothing came I walked toward her. She had on a dark sweatshirt that was missing the "b" from the Abercrombie label and a pair of faded jeans. In spite of the near darkness she wore sunglasses that shielded her eyes. Her hair was drawn into a black rope as if she had just awakened from a long sleep. My gut told me that was far from the case.

"I've been looking for you," I admitted. "I didn't know where you lived. What apartment number I mean."

She nodded slowly. "I'm in one twelve. This building," she said tapping the back of her head against the brick wall.

I waited again, but nothing more was said. So I put my backpack on the ground to sit on top of it and wondered if she even wanted a visitor. There was only one way to find out.

"So you made it through the week," I said. "You didn't miss much."

She shrugged. "Anybody miss me?"

I swallowed hard and scrambled the best I could. "'Course, Curt and I and …"

"And?"

"Mrs. Spoon asked about you," I almost blurted out in relief. At least I had one more name to add to the list.

"Spoon? What did she ask about?"

"How you were. Stuff like that. I said I didn't know because I hadn't seen you. She likes you."

"I've hardly even talked to her. How can she like me?"

I was happy to explain. "She likes the way you write. She says you have a ton of talent. A 'unique voice' to quote her. Part of my punishment was to stay after school with her and help with whatever she needed. She thinks I write okay too."

She lifted off her sunglasses and placed them on the top of her head before replying. "You do. I liked the last thing you did, just like I said in class."

I was going to say thanks, but stopped short when I saw the grey in her face. Even in the shadows it looked as if she hadn't slept in days.

"You don't look so good. Are you okay?"

"Yup," she said. "Just enjoying my time off. It's been a like a vacation on the beach."

She took a pull on the cigarette and blew the smoke high into the air.

It drifted in the breeze until it disappeared in the darkness. "I never knew you smoked," I said. "I mean I never saw you do it before."

She shrugged. "I do it from time to time. Since I have the time." She shrugged again.

"But you'll be back in school soon, right?"

The corners of her lips turned up a fraction of an inch. She didn't laugh but found what I said to be funny. "I guess. Until the next time something happens."

"That sounds so negative."

She stared and measured me up. My neck hairs squirmed before she spoke again. "You think I should be all pumped about going back to school? Like I'll get a standing ovation?"

The anger in her voice surprised me, but I answered back. "No, I wasn't saying that. I know it won't be easy." Then I thought about what she said. "I didn't know you cared so much about what others think."

She stared straight ahead. "I do ... and I don't. It would be nice to just get along sometimes. Instead of just surviving on the scraps thrown my way. Like I'm some kind of dirty mutt."

"I think you're doing as well as you can. Considering

"The circumstances? That I'm trailer trash and my mom is no-where to be found?"

I shook my head and tightened my jaw. "I was going to say considering that you are new here. It takes time to fit in."

She shook her head. "I doubt I'll ever fit in. If it's not Veronica, or Rex, or Vance, it'll be someone else who'll be in my face. Then something will happen again."

"It can't happen again, remember? Mrs. Spoon said one more fight and you'll be kicked out. And you've already had two."

"So then I can't stay in Greendale anymore. I'll just tap my ruby slippers together and find a new school. I hear Mississippi is nice. I've always wanted to eat a catfish. I heard they taste like chicken." She laughed as if satisfied at her joke.

"Now that's a bunch of crap," I blurted. "*This* is your school and you're just as much a part of it as anyone else. Just stay away from trouble." I stopped and tried to lighten the mood. "Anyways, if you leave, I'm stuck with just Curt. You wouldn't make me suffer like that, would you?"

She smiled. Sort of. "He's your bud. You don't need me around."

"That's where you are wrong. I do need you. I've told you more stuff than I've ever told Curt. And I like being around you. Somehow, you just *get* me. Do you understand what I'm saying?"

She studied me and the rings under her eyes seemed to darken. "Do you play Hearts?"

"What?" I asked.

"Hearts. The card game."

I was totally confused but answered the question. "No. Never."

"You should," she said and leaned forward. "It's the only card game my mom ever taught me. Anyways, the idea is to end the game without the Queen of Spades in your hand. If you have it, you lose." She paused. "I have dreams that I'm the Queen of Spades." Her voice lowered. "You're better off without me."

"That is so wrong," I said almost getting angry with her. "On just about every level I can think of."

"No," she disagreed. "I'm not who you think I am."

The wind picked up and her hair flew in the breeze. For the first time I noticed her cheekbones were sharper than usual. She was thinner and it scared me. She scared me even more the way she was talking.

"Then who are you?" I asked. "Just tell me."

"Some other day," she said as she rested her head against the brick. "Not today." She again drew the cigarette to her lips.

A dog barked from somewhere far away and the wind picked up. For the first time that night, I realized how exhausted I was. Then I said one final thing.

"Renee, I'd like to help you."

The corners of her lips again curled a fraction and she looked right through me. But she never said a word.

Chapter Fifteen
Thunder in the Distance

That Saturday morning I woke up after a rotten night of sleep. Renee almost went into a shell after my questions and it was obvious she would rather be left alone. So I did exactly that. I told her I'd come back the next day and we could do something. I had no idea what that would be, but I hoped I could figure out the answer by then.

I looked like hell and felt worse when I entered the kitchen. My mom was still home working on an oversized cup of coffee and punching at the keys on her laptop.

"Jimmy!" she said with some alarm in her voice. "Are you sick? You look terrible!"

"Morning to you too, Mom. And no, I'm not sick."

"Is it all that running? Maybe you're overdoing it."

"No, it's not that at all. I just didn't sleep well."

She closed her laptop, which in and of itself surprised me. She took a small sip and studied me closely. "Is something wrong? At school? " She took a step towards me. "A girl problem? Or maybe, maybe …"

"Drugs?"

"Heavens, no. I know you don't do drugs. I was going to say boys."

"Jeez, Mom! You think I'm gay? That would be worse than doing drugs?"

"No, of course not. At least not to me. But it goes without saying I hope you're not doing either."

"No, Mother," I said with resignation. "I'm not *doing* either." I stared out the window and wished I were a million miles away. She read my face and tried again.

"Jimmy, can we start over?" she asked. I shrugged in response. "Something is bothering you. Why don't you tell me about it?"

I hadn't confided in her since the fifth grade when I told her I peaked on the girls in the gym locker room with a guy named Bruce. We hadn't seen much because there wasn't that much to see besides training bras and white panties. Funny thing was, 'ol Bruce had always wanted to be a priest. After that day he changed his mind and now he's the president of the student council and is fairly close to King Shit. He's into babes big-time and I think I must have played a tiny part in his transformation. Anyways, the fact was it had been a long time since I spilled my guts to her even a little. So when I sat down in a kitchen chair, I gave it one last try.

"Mom, you remember Renee, right?" She smiled one of those "now I get it" smiles that parents throw out every now and again but I blocked it fast. "No, Mom. It's nothing like that."

"Like what?"

"It's not a problem like you're thinking."

"Then what is it?"

I figured I had nothing to lose by talking to her. Or maybe more specifically nowhere else to go. So I continued. "You know she got in trouble for fighting just like I did, right?" She nodded and warmed her hands on the coffee cup. "Well, I went to see her yesterday and I'm really worried about her. She gets in these … these … moods."

She almost waved her hand as if she was shooing away a fly. "All girls have moods," she explained. "It's the nature of the beast of a young girl."

I knew she didn't understand what I was trying to say. "No, it's way more than that. It's like she's two people. One as happy as can be and the other one that is lower than zero. Yesterday she was bad again. I'm really worried about her."

Then she did a strange thing; she nodded like a real mom. Like one who really cared about what I was saying. "Tell me more," she said and narrowed her eyes. "Please."

So I told her what I knew about Renee except for what she didn't need to know. I started with all the crap she had been through for most of her life. About her mom and how she was tramping around the country with a truck driver looking for a major payday. How last night Renee seemed as dark and ugly as a February morning in Wisconsin. When I was done, she stood up and poured herself a new cup of coffee like she was settling in for the long haul.

"Wow," she finally said, "that poor girl. She's been through a lot." She thought for a second. "So she lied to me about having a family who needs a house?"

I nodded. "I guess she had to. Kinda like survival mode."

"I guess." She licked her lips and I could tell she was thinking. "I had no idea it was so bad for her. No one should have to go through things like that. Especially someone so young."

"I know. Even though most times I think she can handle it, it's the other times that worry me."

"I understand what you're saying, Jimmy. Maybe more than you think."

I shook my head in confusion. "What does that mean?"

She took a long look out the patio window at a day that couldn't decide if the sun should break through or it should rain like hell. Then she finally spoke. "You really don't remember, do you?"

"Remember what?" She took another long look into the middle of the coffee cup and swirled its contents. Her fingers took turns alternatively gripping and releasing the cup in a strange rhythm. I finally had to speak again. "Mom?"

"I suppose you should know," she started slowly. "You're old enough." She paused. "Did you ever hear your dad say 'remember the days'?"

"Yes, sure."

"What does that mean to you?"

"I thought he was talking about the good old days like all … umm … old people do."

She smiled. "Thanks for that." Then she got serious again. "What he's referring to is the time when you were only about two or three. I started to act funny, up and down all the time. I would be happy as a lark and clean the place like crazy and then some days I would be too tired to move. I remember a tiredness in my head, a cloud that wouldn't leave."

"I'm not sure what you mean. What was it about?"

"That's the point, Jimmy. It wasn't really about anything. It just was. I battled it for a year or two. Your dad and I almost split up over it."

"You … and dad? Split?" I said in shock.

"Yes," she replied honestly. "He said if I didn't see someone to get help, our marriage would be over. I resisted, of course. But you helped."

"Me?"

"Yes. You were just you," she said as her eyes filled with moisture. "One day you came and lay next to me in bed when I was having a bad day. All you said was that you 'lubbed' me. I cried my eyes out and decided I had to do something. I couldn't live with myself the way I was anymore. Not for me or your father. More than that it was about you. You deserved better. So I went and got help."

I was too stunned to say much. I never expected anything like this and her words sat on the kitchen table like a half-eaten bagel. Only it was my turn to take a bite.

"What did they s … s … say?" I stuttered.

"Back then they called it manic-depressive. Now it's known as bipolar." She was on a roll so I let her keep going. "I went on some medicine and it helped me get normal, whatever that may be. I found exercise helps too. You never wondered why I walk everyday or go to the gym so much?"

"I thought it was all about your thighs to be honest. So that you didn't turn into a ... well, a whale."

"My thighs may have something to do with it," she admitted. "Hopefully I'll never be an exhibit at the Shedd Aquarium. But mostly it helps me stay stable. I never want to go back to that dark place again. I'm not always perfect, but I've been able to manage the condition. At least I think so."

"Wow," I said. "I hardly know what to say. I never knew that you ... you—"

"Were nuts?"

"No," I said. "I was going to say sick."

"You really don't remember, do you?"

"No," I replied. "I sort of remember you being sad. I remember I wanted to get you a puppy to cheer you up because I thought it would help. How dumb was that?"

She teared up again. "No, not dumb. Not dumb at all. In fact it's a rather wonderful thought."

The conversation stopped and allowed us both to regroup. I rubbed my eyes again and as Holden would say it made me aware of how goddam tired I was. But I had enough left to ask one more question about what started the whole conversation in the first place.

"So you think Renee has the same problem?" I asked.

She sipped the last of her coffee and set the cup gently on the table.

"I could never tell you that in a million years, Jimmy. I just sell homes for a living. It's possible she has something much more than just the hot and cold hormones of youth. I can tell you one thing—it sounds like she needs a friend. You may want to keep an eye on her and see how she does."

"You're the second person this week that told me that."

She nodded and ignored her cell phone as it came to life at her side. "She is always welcome here if you guys need a place to hang out. You know that, I hope."

I looked at her as a stray beam of sunlight flickered off her coffee cup.

"Thanks Mom," I said as my eyes locked on to hers. "And Mom?"

"Yes?"

"You know that I still 'lub' you, right?"

She smiled and ignored her phone as it vibrated deep within her holster.

***

The day alternated between periods of sunshine and rain clouds that let go of their load. I went for a short run just to shake things out and got caught in a storm. I always liked running in the rain and even now it brought me back to being a kid. As the rain pelted my face I remembered how I would run through the yard and spin like a top and let the rain wash over my body. Even though I was older now the rainwater still cleansed me to my core.

After the run I showered and chilled the rest of the afternoon. These were the times I wished I had a little brother or sister. I know that some of my friends said their kid brother or sisters were a real pain, but I would take that chance any day of the week. I even hated that we couldn't have a dog because it might leave a microbe or two on the carpet. For the most part I was always alone, except for the damn fish that spent most of their time eating their own poop.

Later I decided to take a walk even though it was bad weather. I was determined to follow through on my promise to Renee and help the best I could. It was my mom's past that made me even more nervous for my friend. I had googled "bipolar" and "mental problems" for an hour and felt even more over my head than when I had started. What did I know about everything Renee was feeling that made me think I could help her? Was I some kind of teenage Freud who could get in her head and straighten it out like cleaning

174

up the crap in the garage? Then another little voice sounded and told me what I needed to hear. *She needs you,* it said. *Don't let her down.* I wasn't some sort of spandex wearing superhero and never would be. I had my own personal landfill-sized pile of doubt and worry that nearly bit me in the ass every day. Still, for the time being I was locked-in on being a better person than I had been the day before. I decided Renee would come first.

I walked toward her apartment and the sky began to darken when more rain clouds moved in. A rumble from the distance echoed and I hoped I wouldn't get caught in the storm before even getting to her place. I picked up my pace and passed an old lady getting walked by her little white poodle. As paranoid as it sounds, more than once I was convinced people laughed at me when I walked on by. But today I was feeling lifted by the good I intended to do that I gave the old lady what I thought was a nice smile. She reacted by looking away as if I was going to steal the little hairball right out from under her nose. *What did I do to deserve that?* I nearly said aloud. Did she have any clue that I was probably more afraid of her twenty-pound furball taking a chunk out of my leg than she should be of me? I shook my head and let her swing as wide as she needed to escape from my threat.

Renee's place was just ahead and I strained to see if she was anywhere in view. The grounds were empty and the only sound was of the metal swings rattling in the breeze like the sound of wind chimes. I headed towards her apartment and pulled at the front door that led to her complex. The building had a set of double security doors that only allowed entrance into each unit by key or buzzer. I hit the one marked one hundred and twelve and waited for a response.

"Yes?" came the static-filled reply.

"I'm looking for Renee," I explained. "My name is Jimmy."

A few seconds passed before the reply came.

"She's not in," said a woman's voice. "She went out to the swings. She likes that."

"She's not there," I offered. "I looked."

"Well, then she ain't there," came a final reply. "If you see her, tell her we left. We had to go to the store."

"Sure," I mumbled. I pulled away from the buzzer and spun to make an exit.

I headed back towards the swings but they were still empty. I checked in the cement tube and found it the same way. The wind was picking up and it drew my attention to the field beyond the small play area. The area was actually a collection of tall weeds and strewn garbage more than an actual field. It wasn't particularly deep; probably no more than fifty yards and it butted up against the railroad tracks running through the middle of the city. I took a small step into the weeds and studied the metal tracks lying in the distance. The railway was abandoned most of the time and was a remnant from a time long ago. It still carried the occasional Amtrak car traveling between Milwaukee and Chicago or freight cars covered with a string of graffiti. The drawings always messed me up because they pulled me out of Greendale into a world I had never seen. A world I guessed was a million times more dangerous than the bubble-wrapped protection I lived in.

I stepped through the weeds and ignored the slap of the stalks scratching against my jeans. I moved toward the tracks and plowed ahead as if some laser beam drew me in. The rumble intensified and warned of a major storm, but I ignored it as best I could. Within a minute I reached the stones at the edge of the train tracks and climbed the hill the wooden railroad ties were buried into. I balanced on one and looked into the distance, but there was no movement in any direction. So I walked north toward a small patch of woods that ran alongside the tracks. Each tie was about three feet apart and I stepped carefully in order to stay on my feet. As I got closer to the woods, I headed toward a pile of broken masonry bricks and tree limbs that looked like an unofficial dumping ground. It was there I heard a sound that reminded me of the cry of a small child, but it was much more than that. It was a voice I knew. One in pain. I ran and jumped over a small pile of rotting grass and saw her lying helplessly.

"Renee!" I shouted and lurched toward her. She was on her left side with her back to me but I had no doubt who it was. Her jeans were pulled down and dirt covered her t-shirt. My head jerked as someone sprang from the tall grass and took off at top speed. I didn't know who it was, but then he turned to look back at what he had left behind. The face was hidden in the shadows of the darkness and I couldn't see who it was. That was until lightning flashed in the sky and told me all I needed to know.

I thought about giving chase but Renee's groan made the decision for me. I crawled in front of her and cleared the hair from her face. My hand smeared the blood running from one side of her nose. I nearly panicked and screamed for help, but knowing no one was near, I did the best I could at staying calm. That stood in contrast to the trembling that appeared on her swollen lips.

"I didn't do anything," she whispered in a hoarse voice. "I was on the swings and he hit me from behind. Then he dragged me."

"It's okay," I reassured her knowing it was anything but that. I held her hand tighter. "Everything is okay." Her eyes glazed and she turned to look in the distance. When the sky rumbled again I told her the truth. "I need to get you to the hospital. Right now."

She gripped my hand so hard I flinched. Then she looked in my eyes.

"Why, Jimmy? Why?"

I had no answer. The fact was I was scared. With her hand still in mine, I was sure she already knew.

Her eyes closed and I didn't even have to try to answer. It was as if a part of her life-force had been extinguished right in front of me but her heart beat against all hope. I cradled her head as the drizzle started. A full-fledged torrent of heavy rain and wind followed and slapped at us like it was sent from an angry god itself. I curled my body around her to protect her from the elements the best I could. With my free hand I called the only person I could think of.

***

My mom arrived within ten minutes and ran toward the swing-set to where I had carried Renee. I didn't say a word, but looked up helplessly. When she saw Renee she put a hand to her mouth.

"Jimmy! What happened?"

I didn't answer and tried to lift Renee back into my arms.

"I'll tell you in the car. We need to go to the hospital." I looked up as the rain beat on my face. "Please, Mom?" I said as much a question as a statement.

She helped me to my feet as I picked up Renee. She was light as a baby and I took a short step toward the car, but stumbled on the wet stone lining the playground.

"Careful, Jimmy," my mom said. "She looks …"

I filled in the blank. "I know, Mom. But she's going to be okay. She has to be. I promised her."

***

The ride to the hospital was short. We went directly to the emergency room and were met by a nurse who asked us the usual questions. Renee was in no shape to say much of anything so I answered for her. They placed her in a bed and she laid back as if she was on her deathbed. I told them everything I could and then cut directly to the heart of the matter.

"I think she was raped," I said finally as I looked the nurse in the eye.

The activity in the room slowed at the power of the word. The nurse froze and my mom's hand squeezed the back of my neck.

"Why do you say that?" asked the nurse. "Did she tell you?"

"She didn't have to. I saw what I saw," I tried to explain. "And I saw someone running away from her."

"Rex," Renee said as she stirred in the bed. "It was Rex."

I nodded at the nurse.

"I'm calling the police," she said and lurched for the phone.

***

The rest of the night was a blur as a series of policemen asked me questions. Renee was taken to an examining room and I didn't see her for the next hour while I was being interrogated. My mom stayed at my side and nodded her head at my story and occasionally rubbed my shoulder in support. I told them what I saw and how I was more than sure it was Rex. The combination of conquest and excitement welded on his face was burned into my brain. Just as much as was the memory of fear and hopelessness carved onto Renee at that terrible moment.

"It was him," I told them. "Damn me to hell if it wasn't."

The emergency room became a whirlwind of activity. Renee's aunt eventually came and ran toward the curtained room acting as her fortress. I sat in a hard-backed plastic chair and waited patiently as my mom took turns drinking coffee and calling my dad to keep him informed. She held my hand more than once and held back from asking more than the bare minimum of questions. Both of which I appreciated and told her so without any words even being spoken. The police left an hour or two after they arrived and I finally had a chance to see Renee. I took a deep breath and stepped behind the white curtain that was her thin barrier to the world. I wasn't prepared for what I would see.

She was lying under a beige cotton blanket drawn up to her chin. Her aunt was sitting in the chair beside the bed and said something, but I have no recollection of what it was. I may have responded, but I can't be totally sure of what I said. I was too focused on the lifeless black eyes that stepped into my world only a short time ago. Renee tried to smile but her swollen lips were already doubled in size and she was barely recognizable. She had an ice pack covering the left side of her face and a bandage taped to the underside of her cheekbone.

"Jimmy," she said in a dreamy voice. "What are you doing here?"

Her aunt gave me a shrug and I knew Renee was feeling the pain medication coursing through her system.

"I just needed to see you," I lied. "To make sure that you'll be okay."

She nodded and licked her puffed lips. Then she smiled a faraway smile that reminded me of my grandma just before she died in the nursing home.

"I'm okay," she said in a whisp of a voice. "These pillows sure are soft. Just like clouds." She looked at me through her fog again.

"That's good, Renee," I said. "You just rest. You'll be better soon," I promised.

"Yes. Better," she said in a voice that mimicked my own.

Then I tried to smile but failed miserably.

Chapter Sixteen
Fallen from the Nest

Renee was released from the hospital the next day. I went to her apartment but her aunt said she wasn't up to seeing anyone. That was almost expected, but I still felt shut off from everything. She explained Renee was sleeping and that I should come by another time. In a day or two, she told me. I promised I would and made her tell Renee I had been by.

At school that Monday I had no idea what anyone knew of the situation but prepared for the worst. I didn't meet Curt that morning and mom dropped me off at the drive-through of the school. She told me to have a good day but if those words were any more hollow they could have held a family of raccoons. I slammed the door and walked into the red-brick battleground that used to be called school.

I pushed through the glass doors and it was like entering a teenage twilight zone. Maybe I was just freaking out, but the faces had morphed into a collection of aliens straight out of *Star Wars.* As the dialogue clicked and whirred around me, I stopped and caught my breath against a locker away from my own.

"Do you mind," said a voice from behind. "I'd like to get into my locker."

I grunted out an unintelligible response and tried to clear my head. Unfortunately, dead in my sights was the sophomore pole housing all of the usual suspects. Veronica stood front and center and glared as I neared. If she could have bottled her anger it would have probably filled a gallon jug. Her eyes widened and she chomped her gum as if she was Cleopatra downing an oversized grape. Lance and a foursome of Billys guarded the perimeter of the pole like it was an entrance to a forbidden land.

"There he is," rose a whisper from the band of Billys. "It's *him!*"

Veronica turned to me and sneered. "Rex is in trouble because of you," she said. "You and that little sleaze friend of yours."

I stopped dead in my tracks and sure as shit my stuttering shadow decided to step front and center. It was the damndest thing, I could be going along as smooth as orange sherbet but the minute I hit a speed bump my brain would overload. It would short circuit to the point that my lips would quiver like they were going to fall from my face like in a Donald Duck cartoon.

"I ... I ... didn't do ... do ..." I sputtered. I caught sight of Vance studying me from the second wave.

"Do, do, do," said a Billy as he mocked me. "Rex didn't do anything either. She was into him and you know it."

"No," I said as I tried to redeem myself. "It wasn't like tha ... that. You weren't there."

"And you were?" asked Veronica. "You know exactly what happened?"

That caught me off guard. I wasn't there for everything but I knew what I saw. At least what I think I saw.

"He was there," I said as strong as I could. "And Renee was lying on the ground. Hurt."

"Maybe whatever happened was mutual. She's no angel you know." She stopped and thought. "You know that first hand, don't you?"

She laughed an ugly laugh but her point was made.

"We're just friends."

"With benefits, obviously. It's probably the same with Rex. Except now she's making up stories."

"She's not," I said even though I was shaking inside. "I know her."

Actually I didn't know her completely but I would never admit that to Veronica and her friends in a million years. As the pressure built on my shoulders like the beams from a ten-story building; I walked by and tried not to fall on my face. In that respect, it was a very successful morning.

***

The rest of the day I heard whispers about the "new girl" and suddenly I became "her boyfriend". I caught wind of what people were saying from some of the guys on the cross country team. They ranged from the whole thing being made up to Renee being bludgeoned to death by some black guy from the city. The last one even resulted in a few jumpy girls wanting to go home in case it was true. Principal Scheel even decided it was crazy enough to make a schoolwide announcement over the lunch hour.

"Good afternoon, everyone," he said. "It has come to my attention that there are many rampant rumors going around the school today. All of which are either completely untrue or totally unsubstantiated. It is true there was an incident involving one of our students is being investigated by the police. Suffice to say, the student is at home recovering for however long it takes. I would also like to say I want all rumors to stop immediately. They are hurtful and will do no one any good. If they continue," he warned, "the offending party will be spending time with me." He stopped to let the statement sink in. "I appreciate your patience and maturity throughout this difficult time. Thank you."

The lunchroom quieted and with my usual paranoia busting out like a weed I felt a million eyes on me. If some of the kids didn't know anything about the "incident" they sure as hell were aware of it now. I chewed my sandwich as nonchalant as I could but the salami stuck in my throat like hot tar. I gagged down the remnants but that was the last piece of lunch I managed.

"Are you okay?" asked Curt from alongside me.

I nodded. "I'll live. At least for awhile yet."

"You didn't do anything wrong, you know. You just helped Renee and did what was right."

I looked him in the eye and was grateful for his support. Thanks, Curt. I know that deep down. Then why do I feel like I'm the one in the wrong?"

"Because of the pressure. You can't see it but it's here with everything you do."

"How do you deal with it?" I asked him. "Sometimes I can hardly breathe."

He shrugged and peeled back a banana. "One morning I woke up and decided to stop caring about what anyone else said. That was the day I got my cowboy boots."

"For real?"

He nodded. "I was at the mall and decided I liked them. That was enough for me."

I looked past his thin mustache and realized I had underestimated him. "I could never do something like that."

"Yeah you could, Jimmy," he said around chews of the banana. "You might be closer to it than you think." Then he paused and looked over the cafeteria. "You won't be a sophomore forever, Jimmy. Someday we'll have our time. It can't rain every day, can it?"

"Curt," I said back to him, "you have the heart of a poet. Who would have thought?"

He shook his head. "I know what I'm good at. Dumb-ass stuff like Lego building and other nerd stuff. Not with words. I think each of us has to find a way at our own pace."

I looked at him and bit my lower lip. Then I understood. "Just like running."

"Something like that. You're a distance runner, Jimmy. You

have to start slow to finish strong." He crushed up his lunch bag and put both hands around it. "Maybe it's the same way in life. He shrugged. "Then what do I know?"

"More than you think, Curt. I hope your right. Because, I feel like I started in last place fifteen years ago."

"You'll get there someday." He looked across the lunchroom before turning back. "You'll be happy to know I'm thinking of ditching my cowboy boots for a pair of high-tops. I keep getting blisters on my heels from the things. I think it's time for a change."

I smiled at my friend. "You keep the freakin' cowboy boots, Curt. Personally, I hate them. But they're you all the way through. When you boil it down that's all that really matters. Right?"

He nodded back. "I guess so, Jimmy. Someday I'll know for sure."

We finished our lunches as the noise of the lunchroom rolled on. Curt even surprised me more that day. Three times he found me and acted like a fullback blocking when we switched classes. I was feeling as alone as my black rock, but he made me believe I could get through the day. *Maybe I am too hard on him*, I thought. He was just a kid like me trying to navigate through a jungle completely unarmed. All the time wearing a pair of butt-ugly cowboy boots I wouldn't wish upon my worst enemy.

"I hope Renee is okay," he said finally after drinking the last of his milk. "She doesn't deserve all this crap." His eyes roved around the cafeteria.

"No she doesn't," I added. "No one does."

***

My next class was with Mrs. Spoon and I hoped it would be a shelter from the storm. When I entered I tried to stand tall, but that faded quickly when a roomful of eyes hovered on me. I slid into my seat and quickly opened a notebook and doodled to pass time. I had the urge to draw a face that eventually took shape as a sort of demented jack o'lantern. I shaded half the face and was planning on completing my masterpiece until Veronica craned her neck for a better view. That broke the spell and I hid the page and waited for Mrs. Spoon to get things going. When the bell rang I sat pencil straight and tried to block the static bombarding my brain in choppy waves.

Mrs. Spoon sat at her desk for nearly a minute and didn't say a word. She looked out the window at a raspberry colored sky and stared at a group of starlings sitting on a nearby tree branch. A gust of wind blew and a few leaves broke free and blew into the distance. Then the birds followed in a choreographed arc the flock had engrained in their DNA for a thousand years. They disappeared into the distance but Ms. Spoon's eyes didn't move a fraction of an inch. She watched a single bird that remained frozen on the edge of a dying branch. The bird was huddled and its feathers ruffled in the strong winds. Its beak opened and closed almost like it was singing a note asking for the sun to reappear. Then without warning its beak stopped moving. Mrs. Spoon looked old at that moment and I clenched my pencil waiting for her to speak. Then she stood up and looked toward the class.

"Life is a difficult thing, is it not?" The class murmured, but I don't think a real word was spoken. I took to doodling again, but focused on what she said. "Sometimes it can be filled with great joy and sometimes great pain. Sometimes maybe even both at the same time." She walked between the rows and the room remained quiet. "Sometimes it's filled with great beauty and other times an ugliness that comes from darkness in our souls. And yet," she said, "we continue on day after day."

"No offense, Mrs. Spoon," interrupted Veronica, "but is this going anywhere? I thought this was a writing class, not extinguishing philosophy."

"Existential philosophy," she corrected.

Veronica's lips set into a pout. "Whatever," she replied. "But you're not talking about writing as far as I can tell."

Mrs. Spoon smiled and nodded her head. Then she took a deep breath as the shine returned to her eyes. "Aha, Ms. Styles, but therein lies the rub! A writer has to experience the lowest of lows and touch the highest of highs. After doing so must let joy and pain stew together until a magical recipe is achieved. There is no perfect formula to become a great writer, but pain and agony must be matched with love and hope until the written page screams forth." She stopped and looked into each student's eyes. "My mentor taught me, just as I will you, that a great writer has the observational powers of a detective, the dedication of a tradesman and the heart of a poet. When all three are conjoined together, brilliance can be attained that will light up the world."

Veronica rolled her eyes and decided to counter. "Maybe some of us don't want to be writers. Is there any problem with that?"

"That is no problem at all," said Mrs. Spoon. "Unfortunately, I think you are missing my point."

"Which is?"

Mrs. Spoon walked back toward her desk then turned to face us. Then she sat on the edge of the faded wooden top and readied to speak. She was interrupted before she even got a word out.

"What she is trying to say, Veronica," said a loud voice from across the room. "Is that a great writer has the ability to make sense of all of the shit in the world. The good and the bad. Maybe even the crap that floats somewhere in the middle. The place where most of us live. How sometimes writing might lead us to a place we can be better than we ever thought possible. To a place we can be who we were meant to be."

The class was silent and Mrs. Spoon looked toward the speaker.

"Thank you, Vance," she said with a surprised look. "I think you understand what I was trying to say. We might use different words to get there. But ultimately we arrived in the same place."

Veronica looked like she could bite the head off a bat and her cheeks turned as red as her lips. She had been stung by one of her own and the class braced for the aftershock. Surprisingly she didn't say anything as she slung down into her chair. For the moment, I was energized like I had swallowed a twelve pack of Duracells.

"I don't proclaim to have all the answers to what makes us tick as humans," Mrs. Spoon said as she leaned forward. "Nor will I ever. Still, it is important that each of us take the time to think about what makes us unique as individuals. Be it on a day that holds darkness or one that holds light. Given recent events, today is a good day to start."

"About what?" asked a voice from the back row.

"About what the word 'truth' means to you." she said. "When it is boiled down to the simple essence of what it is. What you see, smell and taste when you think of that single five-letter word. I'd like for you to tell me in your own words in the next fifteen minutes." The usual groans followed. "This particular assignment will not be graded and even the simplest thoughts will be rewarded as extra credit for those grade conscious individuals."

I shielded my eyes with my hand and looked at the face I doodled and wondered what I knew about truth. I was fifteen years old and hadn't done squat yet. For the most part I lived in the shadows and had found a sort of desperate comfort there. What if I just stayed there? What would become of me? Living my life like an extra in a movie that didn't even get his name mentioned in the final credits? The truth? *You can't handle the truth!* I wanted to shout like some sort of pimply-faced Jack Nicholson. Instead, I turned the page and began to write:

The Truth As I Know It
by
Jimmy Parker

The truth is, before this year I had absolutely no idea what the truth is. I used to say, "It is what it is." Like those words made whatever garbage bag-sized crap somebody stuffed down my throat somehow easier to swallow. The truth is it hurt each and every time and it's only been the last few weeks that I've gotten tired of being a human dumpster.

Now I think that "truth" is as real as this pencil pressing on the paper. It's not always good or bad, but like the perfect note from a violin or the smell of a spring day, it is utterly and completely right. Even if no one else sees the truth the same way as you, it's as if every molecule inside of you lights up and screams, "There it is, you idiot! Can't you see it?" To close your eyes to the truth is a sin against what you can become. Sometimes the truth is hard, but to deny it, is to deny yourself. And that's more than a shame; it is a total waste of the life given to us.

When I was done I sat quietly and returned to my doodling. Only this time, the face evolved into someone I knew.

***

I went to cross country practice that day, but I may as well have gone home and watched some righteous judge demean another inbred idiot on court TV. We ran through the park and I pretty much stayed to myself. The run actually seemed more therapeutic than real training. I guessed I carried the same genes as my mom because every time I was done with a workout my head was miles lighter. But today I had more than myself to worry about. I finished the run by taking the back path through the woods leading to the school. The team was spread out and string of runners stretched over at least a mile. I put my head down to avoid the low-lying branches and was glad I was nearing the end. When I did look up it was to a sight I didn't expect.

"Jimmy, my man," said a deep voice. "You got a second?" The question was more a demand than a request and I stopped on a dime.

I grunted before responding. "Sure," I said and looked at the deserted path behind me. About ten feet in the woods were three more guys I knew only by face. *Seniors*, I thought.

The face with the five o'clock shadow spoke. "It's about you and your friend. To get to the point, nothing better happen to Rex or something will happen to both of you. Something you won't enjoy. Maybe not today or even this week but we promise you'll remember it for the rest of your life. You can tell that little bitch friend of yours the same thing. You hear me, boy?" he said as he stepped back into the woods.

I nodded and started into a little shake as I made my way toward the school. I had no idea what the hell to do next.

Chapter Seventeen
Day of Truth

I didn't say a word to anyone about the guys in the woods because I decided it wouldn't do any good. It wasn't because I was afraid of being a nark, but I figured what were the cops going to do? Assign a bodyguard because I might get beat up two weeks and three days from next Tuesday? I thought they were just words from some of Rex's friends, but if I eventually turned up dented then I was wrong. I was more concerned with Renee and how she was doing, but I still hadn't been able to talk to her.

The police had stopped by the previous day and were supposed to come again that night. As I sat at the supper table waiting my first thought was of the threat occurring only hours earlier. Somehow it already seemed more dream than reality. When my mom led the cops into the kitchen, I sat up straighter in the chair.

"Jimmy, the police have a few more questions for you. Just to make sure of a few things."

"Sure," I mumbled. "I guess."

A pair of policemen quickly hovered over me like blue shirted giants. We did the old school handshake and they dove into their business.

"Jimmy, I'm Detective Anderson and this is Detective Loferski," he said. "We just need a few minutes." The other detective nodded and the sight of their silver badges made me feel like I had to take a major dump. I clenched and just nodded. "We are finalizing our evidence on the incident and we just want to make sure of a few things." He stopped talking and looked at my mom who gave them unspoken consent to continue. We went over the basics for the third time and I told them everything that happened in detail. It was only toward the end of the interview that their interest peaked. "So tell me again what you saw at the railroad tracks. Specifically whom you saw. It is important you are a hundred percent sure. The DNA test is still pending and we may need your testimony to proceed. Jimmy?"

I started to sweat immediately. "I saw Rex from school," I said as clear as I could. "The lightening flashed and it lit him up like a Christmas tree. I saw him running away from where I found Renee. I am positive."

They almost seemed pleased at my statement.

"This case may go to trial if the evidence is strong enough. Your testimony may be vital depending upon the test results. Even more so if things continue as they are."

I was confused and I told him so. "As they are?"

The detectives looked at each other as if they were deciding how much information to divulge. "Your friend has been difficult to interview. She seems to be traumatized and is having, umm, difficulties. Her statements back up what you've told us, but we are still waiting for the lab tests from the hospital."

"Is she okay?" I asked.

"Physically, she is healing up," said Detective Anderson. "But she will need some help to get over this. Things take time."

"What happens next?" asked my mom.

"The DA needs to determine if there is enough evidence to pursue conviction. If he decides there is, charges will be filed. If not, it will be dismissed."

"Dismissed?" I nearly shouted. "No way!"

"It will depend on the evidence, Jimmy. There is no other way," said Detective Loferski.

"So where is Rex now?"

"He is at home and being monitored. He has been instructed to avoid contact with any of the involved parties."

"What about his friends?" I asked.

"Why would you ask that?" asked Detective Loferski. "Has there been any trouble?"

I avoided the answer and my mom looked at me. "Jimmy?"

"Not really," I lied. "I was just thinking about the 'what ifs'".

"What ifs?" my mom repeated.

What if I get my head bashed in, I almost said out loud. "I'll let you know if something happens," I said vaguely.

The detectives measured me up as if they should push a little harder for information. Then they looked at each other and remained silent.

***

I didn't sleep well that night and my dreams alternated between my face getting turned into mashed potatoes and Renee running into the night. Either way I lost. I looked at the ceiling and the light of my screensaver created shadows overhead. I studied the flickering ceiling and let my mind wander to wherever it took me. How had things gone to shit so fast? I mean, a month ago I was just a dweeb sitting at the lunch table and now I was, well … a dweeb with major problems sitting at a lunch table. The guilt rolled in like a hurricane when I thought about Renee and what she was going through. I thought about what she was feeling. I tried to figure out how I felt about her. That one was easier than I thought. Lastly I tossed in bed thinking about the detective's phrase: *She is traumatized and is having difficulties.* So what did that mean? Where did my responsibilities start and end? What the hell should I do about any of it? It was at that moment I got hit by a lightning bolt. The word *Truth* suddenly jumped loud and clear into my gray matter. I decided to give it more than lip service, more than words on lined paper in pencil. I would start to live and do it right. I would do it first thing in the morning. When my screen saver turned to black, I slept well.

***

Morning came and I woke up refreshed. Mom and dad were already gone and I had the place to myself. I did the normal routine and stepped out of the door the same time I did every day. Only today's destination was in a totally different direction than before. School be damned, I was going to see Renee and do what I could to help her. Maybe I could be strong enough to lead her through a terrible time. Maybe I could help her find the way to a new beginning. And maybe, deep down I hoped she would end up being more than a friend to me.

I walked toward her apartment and realized it would be the first day in the short history of my life that I was skipping school. I tasted a freedom I never knew before and walked with a spring in my step. It was only eight o'clock and I doubted Renee was even up yet but my impulse to see her was too strong. The swings behind the complex were empty and swayed ghost-like in the cool morning air. I approached the door leading to her apartment and made my entrance. I hit the button for her unit and waited for what seemed like minutes. It took a second push before I got a response.

"Hello?" said a tentative voice.

The tone was low and almost trembling and it knocked me down a peg. I suddenly worried that I made a major mistake in coming so early.

"This is Jimmy Parker," I said, "and I've come to see Renee."

The pause was long and for a second I thought my words had not gotten through. I was going to repeat them when a buzzer sounded and released the inner door. I grabbed the handle and stepped slowly into the corridor leading to the series of apartments. I counted down the numbers until I reached her door. I cocked back my fist and was ready to knock when the door opened an inch. A metal chain stopped it from opening any further and I saw Renee's black hair. Then the door shut and the chain slid back before it opened all the way.

The air was knocked out of my chest when I saw her. She was as thin as a leaf and her olive complexion was replaced by a color as pale as a communion wafer. The eyes that used to shine were as dull as a fish lying on a pier drawing in its last breaths. If I didn't know better it was like I was seeing her sickly sister. It was Renee, but at the very same time

"Come on in," she said and stepped back. "The place is sort of a mess. I'm supposed to clean it later, but ..." she said as the words hung in the air.

I stepped in and looked around the room. The kitchen sink was filled with dishes and the dripping faucet did little to clear away the grime. The front room was strewn with newspapers and the end table was cluttered with old magazines. Only the empty couch gave the room any semblance of cleanliness whatsoever. Then my attention turned back toward Renee.

"I ... I had to see you," I explained. "I was worried about you. How you were doing."

She exhaled. "Living the good life, as you can see," she said with a wave of her hand.

She was still in what I guessed were her nightclothes: grey sweat pants and a blue t-shirt that nearly hung down to her knees. I followed her toward the front room and I sat on the edge of the couch.

"It's not so bad," I lied. "A roof over your head, right?" I was afraid I gave her a plastic smile, but she didn't seem to notice.

"I suppose," she replied. "I've lived in worse."

"It looks comfortable."

She saw right through me. "Don't kid me, Jimmy. Not today. I know it's a dump. Its home for now. Until ... until, whatever."

Then I made a rookie error in Court of Law 101: Never ask

a question that you don't know the answer to. "Have you heard from your mom since everything happened?"

She sunk back into the couch and it was as if she was an eight-year-old girl again. I saw the pain of a thousand heartbreaks reflect in her eyes and she answered slowly. "No. The last we heard she'd be here after a short trip to Dallas with Melvin. He's the truck driver I think I mentioned. I guess things are going good with him."

I wanted to curse out loud at myself and tried to do a quick three-sixty.

"Your mom doesn't really matter right now, does she Renee? You do. You know you didn't do anything wrong at all. That ass-hole Rex did. I know you'll get through all this shit." I looked at her and wanted to hold her hand, but was afraid to touch her. "I'll help any way I can, you know. Whatever it takes. You're my friend."

She stared straight ahead and for a moment I thought she was watching the morning news on TV. Then she spoke. "I appreciate that, Jimmy. I really do. He'll still get away with it. No matter what happens, he'll always win. It'll be a wound that never closes. Even if they lock him up for a hundred years. Which won't happen."

It came out so forcefully I was unprepared. It was as if her words were written in stone like the Ten Commandments and I had a squirt gun to wash them away.

"You can't think that way," I urged. "Your life is not about what someone did to you. It's about what you can do in your life. Mrs. Spoon says—"

"Spoon," she repeated with more than a little disgust.

"I know she's just a teacher, but she's different. She's smart. She knows about problems and sometimes how they can be helped."

"Maybe. But she's a hundred years old. She doesn't know everything about today."

"No she doesn't. Neither do I. I may be mixed up myself, but

I know what's right," I said as I kept on the offensive. "It's about being true to yourself. It's about using the gifts that you have. Like how you write songs with words that mean something. Things inside of you that no one can ever take away from you."

"Words can't change anything. The same with my stupid songs. They're just words strung in a row like birds on a telephone wire. Just like the birds, they'll be gone when the next train whistle blows and scares them off."

I bit my lip and shook my head.

"You're wrong Renee. No matter what happened in your past, you are different than anyone else I've ever met."

"No," she said as she pushed back into the couch as if she was trying to escape. "I'm not."

"You are," I countered. "Do you remember the first time we met? In the cafeteria?"

"Yes," she said simply.

"You came and sat by me and Curt. Nobody does that. But you did."

"There was no place else to sit," she said with a shrug.

"That's not true. There were a lot of seats left, but you chose us. Maybe there was a reason why." She shrugged again. "You once told me that I think about things a lot. You're right, maybe I think too much sometimes. This may sound weird, but us meeting was destiny. Like somehow we can help each other."

"Destiny," she repeated. "I have no destiny. I just am."

"No," I argued. "You are on the earth for a reason. You just need to find out what it is."

She looked out the small window that opened into the parking lot. Behind that were the swings that rocked in rhythm with the tall weeds in the field. Even further was the edge of the railroad tracks where I found her. I readied to break the spell and draw her attention, but she turned to face me.

"Do you know that kids have been calling to me from outside the window?" She paused when I went blank and didn't answer.

"Terrible and disgusting things. My aunt has called the police, but by the time they get here they're all gone."

"I … I'm so sorry, Renee," I said. "That's just sick. Do you have any idea who?"

She shook her head. "That's the sad thing. I saw a few faces and I don't even know them. I'm sure they're from school." She looked out the window again. "Probably friends of Rex."

"They probably are," I agreed. "Even for what he's done, he still has friends. I guess they believe what they want to believe."

She looked at me and it was as if she had shrunk another size right that second. For all of her tough talk, she was still just a girl. One who was just trying to make it in the world all by herself. One who needed a friend. And one who had been assaulted by a classmate in a field filled with garbage right outside of her own home.

"Do you believe me, Jimmy? I mean about getting raped?"

I didn't hesitate. "Yes," I said and looked her in the eye. "I do."

She nearly teared up instantly.

"The police don't seem so sure. I've talked to them three times already. It's like they think I'm lying."

"They're just making sure, I think. The charges are serious. They came to see me too."

"You?"

"It wasn't a big deal. Just to go over everything one more time."

"What did you tell them?"

"What I saw. That you were hurt. And …"

"And?"

"That I saw Rex running away from the railroad tracks. I guess they wanted to make certain I really saw what I saw."

She stiffened like a frozen pine tree in the dead of winter. For the first time I noticed the depth of the dark bags under her eyes. "It was him. He was on top of me when I woke up." She turned away. "He's so strong. I tried to fight him off," she said with a shaking voice. "His hands were all over me. Touching me. Holding me down. I knew what he was thinking." She started to shake

198

but didn't stop. "He wanted to shut me up. I knew he wanted to hurt me because it made him feel good. He was … he was so *dark* inside I felt sick just touching him. I screamed as much as I could … but no one heard me! Nobody came!" She put her head in her hands and started to cry. I had heard a hundred people cry before, but none like this. It was a mournful wail from a dying animal caught in a trap more painful than I could ever imagine. I wanted to hide so that I could avoid the intensity of the moment, but a second later I was embarrassed by my reaction to her suffering. *She's going to need a friend,* mom and Spoon's voices echoed in my brain. I sat up straight and placed my hand in hers. I felt more intense than I ever did before but right then I couldn't put it into words. Renee did it for me.

"Don't Jimmy! Don't you love me!" she said and pulled her hand from mine. "I don't want anyone to love me!" she shouted in a voice mixed with anger and disgust.

I sat frozen in time and space.

***

I left Renee's house minutes later. I walked as if clubbed by a baseball bat and my head swirled in fifty directions. I had no idea what to say or do anymore and had never felt so lost. I had wanted to make things better, but realized maybe I had only screwed them up. *It was so damn unfair*, I wanted to scream. Then again I knew fair had nothing to do with it. Life gave and life took. Lately I was so far on the wrong side of the ledger that I wondered if I would ever break even again. Not knowing what else to do, I just walked and did my best to keep on breathing.

I made my way to school for second hour and melded into the mass of students like it was another day. I got more bullshit comments from kids that echoed the day before. "Loser. Liar. Asshole," they called me to my face and behind my back. *How could they protect a rapist?* I wanted to ask all of them right back. Did they realize what he had done to her? Did they even have a clue? Was it so important to protect a popular kid that Rex could do anything as if he was entitled to it? I had no answers, but deep down I was as sick as I had ever been. When Renee cried that morning, I could magnify my shitty feelings a hundred times to get to the level of how she felt. I was so out of it all day that instead of sitting at a desk, I may as well have been on the moon.

"Jimmy?" said Spoon later from the front of her class. "Do you have anything to add to the discussion?"

I had no idea at all what she was talking about. It could have been about the last time I scratched my nuts for all knew. So I faked the best I could.

"No, Mrs. Spoon. Not really."

She nodded and moved on and I looked out the window at the birds that came and went.

***

I had told Renee I would meet her after school at her apartments. I wanted her to get some fresh air and she sort of agreed she would go outside with me. Maybe that would be the first step back into the world, I thought. But back to what? I was too worn to really think about the answer and only wished for the best.

After the final bell, I headed out the front doors and walked as fast as I could. I was going to skip cross country and told Curt to tell the coach I was sick. He looked at me weird, so I faked a cough and he rolled his eyes. All the same, I knew he would cover for me.

The day was one of those Wisconsin days that warned of the season ahead. The sky was filled with corkscrew clouds that mixed white and grey like an ice cream cone from Dairy Queen. When the high sun was blocked, it dropped about ten degrees in a heartbeat. I looked up and could see dark clouds approaching from the north and sped up.

Renee's apartment building stood in the distance and I recognized her window. I was anxious to see her and hoped I could help her deal with everything delivered her way. She had read my mind and knew how I felt, but for once I didn't even care. So she knew I loved her. So what? There were worse things in the world and I could deal with rejection one more time. This time it wasn't about me.

I sped up my walk and was pretty sure I could get her out of her funk even if I had no clear idea how. I slowed when I approached her building and out of habit took a look toward the small park. But it was the oversized cement tube that made me stop and stare in drop-mouthed amazement. Scrawled in three-foot letters for the entire world to see was a single word. "*Slut!*" screamed the tube in thick, black spray paint. I was too stunned to think but the creak of the swings drew my attention. Renee was toeing the ground while fixating on the defaced object. Even from the distance, there was a vibration of something terribly wrong. Her hair was like a gnarled root and hung down to partially cover her face. She had changed into a pair of ripped jeans and in spite of the cool day wore only her usual plain white t-shirt. She didn't see me, but looked hypnotized by the word that nearly hung in the air under its own vile power.

The wail of a train whistle woke her from her trance. She looked back toward the tracks and stood up from the seat of the swing. Then she turned and ran toward the sound.

"Renee!" I yelled with a wave of my hand.

The sound of another blast of the whistle drowned out my call.

"Renee!" I screamed again. I dropped my backpack and took off at a dead sprint. I ran harder than I ever had before; only this was the first time it really mattered. There was a fifty-yard gap between us that seemed as if it was a mile, but I vowed I would get to her somehow. I closed the distance step by step, but Renee was determined to reach her destination. I ran by the swings and the tinkle of the chains filled the air. I hit the weeds and the rocky footing caused me to stumble, but I stayed on my feet. I called again, but I might as well have been shouting to someone that was deaf. In some ways, maybe that's exactly what it was.

I was halfway through the field when Renee reached the railway. She climbed up the small embankment and reached the middle of the tracks. Then she looked down the metal rails that disappeared into the distance and into the light of the oncoming train. The rumble of the train got louder and the whistle screamed its alarm. The squeal of brakes cried out as the driver attempted to stop the inevitable. I waved my arms and the sound of my voice echoed in my ears.

"Renee, no!" I screamed loud enough to sear the flesh from my throat.

It did nothing. Renee stood like a statue with her arms spread wide and her t-shirt hanging to her thighs. The light of the oncoming train made her glow like an apparition. I reached the embankment seconds before the train bore down on her. Just before it struck her, the angry whistle sounded one last time.

Her body flew toward the opposite side from where I stood. The train was not a long one, but the seconds seemed like years. The graffiti-laced train cars rolled on in spite of the grinding of the brakes. I wanted to somehow climb over the train but instead was forced to stand and wait. Wait to see what was on the other side. And wait to find a friend that had taken my entire life to find.

The train crawled to a stop and I ran around the back hoping it was all some sort of a cruel joke. Somehow, I half-expected to see her smiling face on the other side like it was all a gigantic mirage. But deep down, from a place I never want to visit again, I awaited the worst.

I saw her at the bottom of the embankment. She was lying on her back and her chest rose and fell with ratchet-like breaths. I stumbled over the railroad ties and made my way towards what was left of the Renee I knew. I leaned over and her black eyes stared at me. A trickle of blood seeped out of the corner of her mouth and her breath came in short gasps. Her cloudy eyes struggled to focus and a trace of a smile was etched on the corners of her lips. I took her hand and she smiled a sad smile.

"Jimmy," she said in a whispered voice. "You're here."

I swallowed before I could say anything.

"I'm here, Renee. I'll always be here for you."

A line of blood appeared on the corner of her mouth. "I'm sorry, Jimmy," she said. "About everything." Then her breathing got thicker. "And before. I didn't mean what I said."

I squeezed her hand harder.

"You really do love me, Jimmy? Don't you?" Then she smiled as a tear ran from the corner of her eye.

I nodded as my vision started to get blurry and she spoke her last words.

"Did you see the light, Jimmy?" she whispered as the blood garbled the words. Then the partial smile froze on her lips and the heaving in her small chest stopped. When her hand went limp in mine, she was gone.

I stood guard over her and had never been that helpless. I wanted to call out, but my voice was frozen. I felt a million things at once, none of which I could explain much less understand. My heart was tearing from my chest and I became an empty and pathetic shell of a human being. Then I broke down as if I was being tortured by a sadistic madman for the sake of his bloodthirsty needs. I screamed at the heavens until my throat became a raw passageway of sound spewing grief toward the heavens. Then a single tear dropped from my eye and mingled with the stream of blood that covered her face. I tried in vain to catch my breath and brushed a tangle of dark hair from her forehead and tried to say goodbye to my friend.

"You're home now, Renee," I said as my vision clouded. "You're home.

***

The rest of the day was a blur. The train conductor called nine-one-one and the emergency crew arrived within minutes. I held Renee's hand and wished for a thousand different things. Most of all, I wished I could have saved her. I hadn't and fair or not, I blamed myself for what happened. Maybe I shouldn't have left her alone that day. Maybe I could have talked to her and helped in some unknown way. Maybe I could have run faster and got there in time to save her. And maybe I could have made her realize how special she was. Now there was nothing I could do to bring her back.

I told my story over and over again to the same detectives that were at my house. I didn't even cry anymore, I suppose I was in shock. Eventually I was ready to leave the police station but before I did, Detective Anderson told me one final thing.

"The DNA sample from the assault came back positive. Charges will be filed against the boy in the morning. I thought you should know," he said.

"Will there be enough to convict him?" I asked. "I mean, now that Renee is … is …"

He didn't make me finish. "Yes. With your identification of the suspect we have a very good chance." He stopped and looked around the room. "I shouldn't be saying this, but one of your classmates came in after he heard what happened to Renee. He informed us that the suspect had bragged before the assault of what he planned to do. The boy even texted your classmate after he did it. I believe the accused will be serving time very shortly."

"Can I ask who came forward?"

"I can't say," he said. "That is confidential."

I nodded and stood up to leave the interrogation room. My parents were just outside the door and my mom was crying. Even my dad looked like he was ready to bust a gut. Then they both stepped forward and put their arms around me.

"We love you, Jimmy," my dad said as clear as could be.

I choked up and hugged them harder.

"I love you too," I echoed as we remained locked. When I felt the warmth of their bodies, I was about two years old again. And it felt good.

We walked toward the exit and I saw a face I did not expect. Talking to another set of officers was Vance. He looked tired and tight-lipped and turned his attention away from them when he noticed me. Our eyes locked and I waited for one of us to flinch. Then he nodded at me and his lips parted slightly. "Hey, Jimmy," I think he tried to say. I nodded back and a rush of relief gushed from me like a fountain.

"Is that a friend of yours, Jimmy?" my mom asked.

I thought about that before I answered. "I think so, Mom. I think so."

Chapter Eighteen
Black Opals

Renee's wake and funeral was two days later. I stayed out of school and took what my doctor called a mental health break. First time the freakin' doctor did something right since the day I met him. The time off let me think about everything, but I still couldn't make sense of most of it. I did some writing and found it helped ease my mind a little. I even finished reading my book. I came to realize goddam Holden was one screwed up kid. Somehow it made me feel good that I wasn't the only one in the world that had a hell of a time figuring things out. Maybe someday I would understand how things worked, but for now, I would just make my way the best I could.

The funeral home was nearly empty that night. Renee's aunt and her family were there along with a few people that probably read about her accident. I heard her mom couldn't be found and they needed to proceed without her. That was just about par for the course, as my mom would say. I looked at the sign-in book and saw a few kids had come before I got there. I didn't blame them for staying because it was pretty hard to look death in the face when you were only fifteen. I waited behind the rows of chairs and tried to slow the beating of my heart when a voice interrupted my thoughts.

"Jimmy," said Curt as he came from behind. "How are you?"

I know he was just being nice because there was no possible way I could answer that question truthfully. So I just shrugged.

"Okay, I guess. As good as you could expect."

"Hello, Curt," said my mom as she and my dad laid a hand on his shoulder. "We're so sorry about your friend. We wish we could have known her better." Curt mumbled something and smiled a little bit. My mom patted him a few times and started to move away. "We're going to sit awhile," she said as the two of them found nearby chairs.

I nodded at them as they moved away.

"It's nice your parents are here," Curt said.

"Yes," I agreed. I had thrown them to the wolves more than once, but not today. "They've helped as best they know how. I mean making sense of everything."

"I think that's impossible. How do you make sense of something that never should have happened?" He paused. "I certainly can't."

I nodded in agreement. "You're right. I can't either. Another side of me says I have to try and find some silver lining out of this or I'll go freakin' crazy." I stopped and then said something that had been eating at me the moment Renee died. "I feel like her dying was my fault. Maybe not all, but a big part of it. I mean I got in the Gritch and all that. Maybe, maybe …"

"That's bullshit!" Curt said loud enough to turn a nearby head. "Totally. You got in over your head but you can't control a guy like Rex. For that matter you couldn't control Renee. She made her own decisions. That's what made her who she was in the first place." He looked toward the casket. "In the end she made the worst decision anyone can ever make."

I blinked and a wave of heat hit me. "I guess. I'll always feel responsible to some degree. Always."

He nodded. "Things will fade and get better. Give it time."

Time I had, I thought. I wished some of it could be with Renee but that was now one more misplaced and unattainable dream.

Then Curt stood tall and looked me in the eye. "You're a good person, Jimmy." He patted me on the back. "If you need anything let me know."

I probably liked Curt more that instant than I ever had before.

"Sure thing, Curt," I promised. "You can count on it." Then he stepped forward to confront the uncomfortable fact that we were moving toward a place that left childhood far behind.

I stood in the back of the room and watched a few people come and go. My parents got up from their chairs and went up to pay their own respects. When they finished they came to me and I told them I needed more time. I moved into an open seat to sit quietly by myself for a few minutes. I stared straight ahead until someone sat beside me.

"Jimmy, can I talk to you for a minute?" Vance asked in a smaller voice than I had come to know.

I looked at him out of the corner of my eye and replied. "Of course," I said. I tried to act as if I wasn't surprised, but the truth is I was. "Vance," I tried to say as evenly as I could. "I … I didn't expect to see you here."

He sat down and looked ahead. "I suppose so." He looked around the funeral home. "It's kind of sad that more of the school isn't here."

I nodded and thought for a second then blurted out what was on my mind. "It was you that went to the police about Rex, wasn't it?"

He tightened. "Yes, but I haven't advertised it yet, if you know what I mean." I understood the predicament he was in and what he was saying to me without actually saying the words. "What he did to Renee was so wrong. No one deserves what he did to her. Not ever."

"I miss her already," I admitted. "She was my friend. She was—"

"Special," he finished. He looked at the little holy card that contained a prayer. "I always wanted to get to know her better. From the moment I saw her, I thought she was beautiful." He turned quickly toward me. "Sorry, Jimmy. I mean if you and her …"

I helped him out. "No, we weren't like that. At least not yet." I thought of our eyes meeting at the police station. "So what happens to Rex?"

"I don't know. He was sort of my friend," he said. "Then again, he wasn't. I was just sort of in the clubs, you know? Because I play football and all," he explained. "Everybody expects things. But after a while the helmet felt more like a noose."

"That bad?"

"For me, yes. So from now on, I'm going solo."

"Solo?"

"You know. From the Billys and the Gritch thing and all. Sometimes I hated who I was becoming. Then when it … it happened, I decided it was way past time."

"Past time for what?" I asked somewhat confused.

"To be who I am, not who everyone *thinks* I am."

I was caught off guard. "That's funny," I admitted. "For a while I would have given anything to have people think I was a guy like you." I watched my parents shake hands with Renee's aunt as they said the hardest words a person ever has to say. I paused and spoke again. "Life is messed up sometimes."

"More than anyone ever told us," he agreed. He took a deep breath. "I'll see you at school, Jimmy," he said as he stood up.

"Yeah, I'll see you." He nodded and walked away.

I sat a long time until I mustered up the nerve to stand up. I took a few steps but before I got to the end of the chairs, Mrs. Spoon met me head on.

She smiled. "I was waiting for the right moment to talk to you. You looked pretty deep in thought. I saw you talking to Vance."

"Yes, he came by." I couldn't help, but replay our conversation. "Turns out he's not so different than me."

"You'd be surprised what some students keep wrapped up inside. Some of it good, some of it …" She left the statement drift.

"I've been having trouble lately with knowing who the good guys are. People are so … so …"

"Confusing," she said to fill in the blank. Then she looked to the front. "I came to pay my respects to Renee."

"That's nice of you," I mumbled out. "She liked your writing class."

She nodded. "Renee was a rainbow of promises. I only wished I would have known her better."

"That seems to be a common sentiment." She looked at me quizzically, but I didn't explain.

"She wrote something the first day of class I thought you should see." She handed me an envelope. "Just don't tell anyone I gave it to you or I may lose my job."

"So you're staying?"

"What else am I going to do? Take up making quilts or scrapbooking? I think I'll stay until they send me to the retirement home."

"You'll never get old. That would be an impossibility."

"Thank you, Jimmy." She looked at the casket. "I'm going to go now. See you in school soon?"

"See you in school," I said as I fingered the envelope.

When she moved away, I opened the envelope and unfolded the paper. And I read:

Girl Bites the Big One

Renee Wizenson, fifteen years young, died today of unnatural causes. Wizenson, who just moved to Greendale from Goat Junction, Nebraska, succumbed to a rare case of "Swollen Brain" induced by excessive worrying. Cool on the outside, Wizenson was known to be a jumbled mass of confusion only to herself.

Though only a teen, Wizenson had lived in eight different states as her mother dragged her from one nameless town to the next. Forming few lasting friendships, Wizenson often latched onto those who accepted her on a no questions asked basis. Known to be a classic underachiever to a parade of teachers, Wizenson likened her life to that of a giant sunflower yearning for the sun. Reaching forever higher, but never actually reaching the ultimate prize.

Wizenson will be cremated so that gawkers cannot comment on how nice her bloated remains look. Her mother will greet the attendees at Morty's Mortuary - if she remembers to show up. Donations are discouraged and any money earmarked for Wizenson should be spent at Wendy's on a chocolate Frosty.

Life gives you no promises, just breaths until they run out.

Renee Wizenson

I studied the curves of her penmanship and signature. At that instant I didn't know whether to cry or laugh. So I did neither. Then I refolded the letter and waited for Spoon to finish her silent prayer. When she left, I took a series of slow steps forward toward the front. Her aunt had decided on an open casket and this was the first time I was at a funeral with one of those. It was hard not to think of some horror movie where the dead person jumps up and scares the shit out of you. I was going to make my parents promise me that if I croaked before them, they would cook me and toss my ashes into the wind. Even better I wanted them to get a helicopter and dump my fried remains over all the running trails in Whitnall Park. That way I would get stuck in the treads of all of the runners and keep moving forever.

I made my way to the casket and a rocket could have gone off and I wouldn't have heard it. I was like a zombie as I neared the felt-lined box. Before I even had the guts to look at Renee, I knelt at the kneeler. Then I looked in. I heard how everyone said the dead person looked at peace and somehow that's what I expected. She wasn't at peace to me, she was just dead. And the body lying there wasn't her at all. She had been full of life and mystery and unexpected discoveries since the day I met her. Now that was over. Her dark hair was parted down the middle and lay motionless on the white backing. She was in a dress that I'm sure she would have said she wouldn't be caught dead in. In God's own twisted irony, she was. Her olive skin was pasty and the mortician had applied a handful of make-up she didn't even need. Worse than that was her eyes were closed. Those iridescent black opals that shined like a pair of buffed marbles were forever closed. I reached into my pocket to lift out a final gift for her. My hand caressed the object and I placed it on the pillow alongside her head. The rock that I found on the beach blended in with her black hair as if it had once been a part of her. The stone settled deep within the pillow and caught the muted lamps with enough light to cast a reflection in my eyes. I let the brilliance wash over me for as long as I could. Then I touched her hand and let myself feel.

Paul Maurer is a graduate from Northwestern College of Chiropractic and currently practices as a Doctor of Chiropractic. He also holds degrees from the University of Wisconsin in Business Management and Marketing.

Maurer has produced multiple marketing materials for both private and corporate use. In addition he has created short stories, song lyrics and a full length middle grade reader and murder/mystery novel. A sampling of his work is available at www.PaulMaurerBooks.com

He resides in Oak Creek, Wisconsin with his wife of twenty-five years, three sons and new puppy. The young adult novel, Touched, is his first published work.

CPSIA information can be obtained
at www.ICGtesting.com
Printed in the USA
FSOW01n1152250816
24195FS

9 781614 690351